He move...
with rem...

"It damned near killed me to leave you," he admitted, his voice rough.

She read the truth of his words in his eyes. This strong, courageous man had exiled himself to keep her safe. And he didn't believe he deserved her now.

"I'm not asking for forgiveness," he continued, his voice somber. "I'd do the same again. And you're right to despise me. I don't expect that to change. But for God's sake, Maya, don't *ever* think I didn't want you."

And then he lowered his head and kissed her—softly, tenderly, as if expressing what he couldn't say.

She savored the sensual heat of his mouth, inhaled the intriguing scent of his skin. He angled her chin, parted her lips with his tongue, igniting a tempest of need in her blood.

He ended the kiss, but didn't move. His uneven breath battled with hers. And raw need blazed in his eyes.

"Maya, walk away," he rasped.

She trembled, knowing she should do it. The past was gone. They had no future together. This was a line they shouldn't cross.

Dear Reader,

I've always been intrigued by the Himalayas, an exotic, mystical land filled with ancient cultures and religions, home to the most majestic peaks on earth. So what better place to end THE CRUSADERS trilogy than Romanistan, a fictitious country located high in that sacred terrain?

I loved learning about the Himalayan cultures while researching this book, and especially liked writing about Maya and Deven, two noble and courageous people. Maya dedicates herself to rescuing downtrodden women and giving them the hope and love she never had. Deven, a man haunted by dark secrets, gave up the woman he loved to save her from evil. Neither expects to embark on a dangerous journey to fulfill an ancient prophecy—a journey that will test their courage, reveal their identities, and enable them to find the love they deserve.

I've taken great liberties with history while writing this series, but the story of the Roma is roughly true (although the royal line and artifacts are my invention). I'm sure I haven't done justice to the cultures involved, but I've had tremendous fun writing THE CRUSADERS. I hope you enjoy the conclusion!

Gail Barrett

GAIL BARRETT

The Royal Affair

Silhouette®
Romantic
SUSPENSE

SILHOUETTE BOOKS

ISBN-13: 978-0-373-27671-4

THE ROYAL AFFAIR

Copyright © 2010 by Gail Ellen Barrett

Recycling programs for this product may not exist in your area.

This edition published by arrangement with Harlequin Books S.A.

For questions and comments about the quality of this book please contact us at Customer_eCare@Harlequin.ca.

Visit Silhouette Books at www.eHarlequin.com

Printed in U.S.A.

Books by Gail Barrett

Silhouette Romantic Suspense

Facing the Fire #1414
Heart of a Thief #1514
To Protect a Princess #1538
His 7-Day Fiancée #1560
The Royal Affair #1601

*The Crusaders

Silhouette Special Edition

Where He Belongs #1722

GAIL BARRETT

Gail Barrett always knew she'd be a writer. Who else would spend her childhood grinding sparkling rocks into fairy dust and convincing her friends it was real? Or daydream her way through elementary school, spend high school reading philosophy and playing the bagpipes, and then head off to Spain during college to live the writer's life? After four years she straggled back home—broke, but fluent in Spanish. She became a teacher, earned a master's degree in linguistics, married a Coast Guard officer and had two sons.

But she never lost the desire to write. Then one day, she discovered a Silhouette Intimate Moments novel in a bookstore—and knew she was destined to write romance. Her books have won numerous awards, including a National Readers' Choice Award and Romance Writers of America's prestigious Golden Heart.

She currently lives in western Maryland. Readers can contact her through her Web site, www.gailbarrett.com.

To my sons, Joe and John K.,
with hopes that you follow your dreams!

Acknowledgment

I'd like to thank the following people for their help:
Frank Henderson, for his information about helicopters;
Lisa Sullivan for her invaluable insights about India;
Ruchi Dahal for answering my endless questions about
Nepal; and as always, Judith Sandbrook, my fabulous
critique partner. Thank you, all!

Chapter 1

Someone *was following her.*

Maya Chaudry pressed herself deeper into the dimly lit alcove, hardly daring to breathe. Cold sweat beaded her palms, and her pulse raced in haphazard spurts. She locked her gaze on the staircase behind her, struggling to hear above the dull roar rocketing through her skull.

Muted sounds drifted up from the ballroom—the high strains of the stringed *sarangi,* the deeper drumming beats of the *mandal.* Bursts of tinny laughter from the women Singh had flown into his Himalayan palace for the lavish affair.

The party was signature Singh—white truffles, vodka filtered through a hundred diamonds, Almas Iranian caviar served in twenty-four-karat gold tins. No cost spared to create that veneer of elegance and sophistication.

And mask the depravity underneath.

Maya's belly clenched, and a fierce sense of urgency tore through her nerves. She had to hurry. She needed to find the kidnapped girl and whisk her to safety before Singh tired of the party downstairs.

But she hadn't imagined those footsteps.

Had Singh spotted her? Had he expected her? A flurry of dread swirled through her at the thought. But breaking into the notorious criminal's palace had been easy—far too easy, the security around the servants' entrance too lax. And now someone was dogging her steps—hiding, biding his time, toying with her in a cat-and-mouse game that could lead to a deadly trap.

She clasped the good luck charm she wore around her neck and forced back the frenzy of nerves. The danger didn't matter. She had to risk it. It was her fault Gina had been kidnapped. In her rush to get the feverish girl to a doctor, she'd broken her ironclad rule and ventured from her women's shelter during the daytime, instead of waiting for the security of night.

And now it was up to her to make this right.

She jerked her gaze to the door at the end of the hallway, sucked in a steadying breath. Then she gripped the hem of the sari she'd lifted from the caterers' truck and dashed across the rug in the hall. Her heart thundered as she raced toward the doorway. Adrenaline pounded her veins. She reached the door, glanced back at the still-empty hallway, then pressed her ear to the heavily carved wood.

Silence. She inhaled, forcing herself to breathe through the choking tension, then quietly twisted the knob.

Light from the wall sconce spilled through the doorway, casting a silver haze over the rug. She crept inside the suite, her steps muffled on the thick Persian carpet, and paused to let her eyes adjust.

A deep hush pulsed in the shadows. The fine hairs on her nape stood on end.

A footstep came from behind.

She gasped, whipped back, but a man slammed into her side. She fell, smacked into the carpet, a sharp cry wrenched from her lungs.

The man landed atop her. She groaned at the violent impact, twisting as his weight crushed her hips. She had to get herself free!

He reached for her wrists, but she went for his armpit, ramming her stiff thumb into his flesh. He grunted, jerked off balance and she instantly rolled to her knees. But he tackled her again, shoving her facedown into the rug, knocking the breath from her chest. Then he grabbed her wrists and locked them over her head.

She squirmed, bucked, fought to heave him off her back, unwilling to let him win. But he was too heavy, too strong. He stretched himself over the length of her and pinned her down with his weight.

He was smashing her ribs, her lungs. Panicked, she butted her head back, but he dodged the move and swore. She lunged sideways, managed to twist her head and tried to bite his arm. But he had the advantage of weight. He shifted forward and trapped her head, then clamped his other hand over her mouth.

Her head grew light from the unyielding pressure. Bright spots danced in her eyes. She raked his palm with her teeth, but he tightened his hold even more.

"Stay still," he warned, and his gruff voice rasped in her ear. She squirmed again, frantic to dislodge him, but his muscled body locked her in place. "Don't move, or I'll have to hurt you."

She tried to nod, to make him loosen his hold, but she couldn't move her head. He crushed her into the rug, turning her arms numb. His brute force bulged out her lungs. She desperately struggled to inhale, but his huge hand blocked off her air.

Then, mercifully, he rolled away.

She wheezed, but breathing was like inhaling fire. She coughed, unable to catch her breath, and gulped air to her searing lungs.

He'd nearly killed her.

And she wasn't out of danger yet.

Her head reeling, knowing she had to act fast, she fought her way to her knees. But the room twirled, and her stomach heaved. She lowered her head, pressed her trembling palms to the rug, waiting for the dizziness to pass.

Running would be futile. As fast as her assailant was, she'd never make it past the door. But she couldn't afford to get captured. She had to find Gina and whisk her to safety fast.

The man snapped on a lamp, and the bright light flooded the room. She blinked, pushed herself from the thick rug and struggled to rise.

But he strode back, grabbed her arm and hauled her to her feet. Still shaking, her temper rising at being manhandled, she jerked her arm from his grip. She straightened her twisted sari, lifted her chin to meet his eyes.

Dark, familiar eyes.

Shock shuddered through her. Her lips parted in disbelief.

Deven Kapur.

He was the last person she'd expected to find at Singh's estate.

She shook her head, as if to unscramble her vision, certain she'd made a mistake. But her eyes hadn't lied. It was Deven, all right. A woman never forgot the man who'd taken her virginity and then dumped her, no matter how many years had passed.

He was taller now, more muscular. His thick, blue-black hair was shorter, the angles of his cheeks more pronounced. But he still had that golden skin, those dark slashing brows, that wickedly sensual mouth.

Her heart made an unsteady beat.

She scowled at her body's reaction, still stunned by how he had changed. The years had hardened his features, whittling the warmth out, paring them down to the stark masculinity underneath. And a scar now jagged through his beard shadow, warning of violence, danger.

He'd been a gorgeous teen—edgy and wild, radiating raw sexual energy. Girls had flocked to him, unable to resist his allure.

He looked far more lethal now.

His wide shoulders stretched the seams of his T-shirt. His biceps bulged as he folded his arms. And he towered over her, that brutal scar menacing, his eyes sparking barely leashed ire.

She had to fight the urge to step back.

"What are you doing here?" His deep, gravelly voice vibrated with outrage.

Her own temper stirred. She didn't owe this man anything, certainly not an explanation—especially if he now worked for Singh.

The thought staggered her. The boy she'd loved had battled for justice, fought for the side of right. She'd never dreamed he'd join forces with her archenemy, the despicable human trafficker and international arms dealer, Sanjeet Singh.

But twelve years had passed since she'd seen Dev, and he was no longer that boy. He was a man—a hard, dangerous man from the looks of him. A man she knew nothing about.

And thanks to a childhood spent on Kintalabad's mean streets, she knew the depths to which men could sink.

"None of your business," she told him, and stepped away.

"The hell it isn't." He grabbed her arm and yanked her back.

Her face hot, she wrenched her arm from his grasp and shot him a level stare. No one intimidated her, no matter how formidable he seemed.

But Deven only moved closer, so close that his warm breath brushed her face, and the heat from his hard body enveloped hers. He loomed over her, dominating her vision, her space.

"I asked what you're doing here, Maya."

"And I told you it's none of your—"

"You made it my business when you climbed that staircase. Now what are you up to?"

His hard jaw flexed in a sign of temper. His dark eyes drilled into hers. She inhaled to regain her composure, but his enticing male scent washed through her, that once familiar blend of soap and man.

And before she could block them, the memories swept back—a hot, steamy night. Whispered words and frantic need. Pleasure—fierce, shocking pleasure—more explosive than she'd ever dreamed.

And despite the danger, despite her anger, she felt something shift inside her, something she'd buried for twelve long years. The insidious warmth of desire.

She stifled it fast. She'd believed him once—believed his promises, his words of love. *His lies.*

And she refused to make that mistake again. She knew better than to trust him—or anyone in this city seething with treachery, corruption and spies. Her success as the Leopard, leader of the underground network that rescued women trafficked through the Himalayas, hinged on astuteness and stealth.

But then a whimper cut through the silence. *Gina*. Pushing aside thoughts of Deven, she spun around and scanned the room—the Hindu murals painted on the walls, the chandelier glittering with crystals, the ornately sculpted Ming chairs.

And in the corner, an open door.

Her pulse accelerating, her hopes rising, she hurried across the room. She paused in the doorway, reached around and flipped on the light switch, spotted the young girl huddled on the floor.

Her heart thudded. "Gina."

She rushed over, and the girl looked up. Her eyes were bloodshot and glazed with fever, her face sweaty and flushed. "Maya?"

"I'm here." She knelt, pressed her hand to the girl's forehead, inhaling sharply at the fiery heat. Her people had rescued Gina in Romanistan's mosquito-infested lowlands, where the girl had contracted malaria—and without medical help, she could die.

Not that Singh cared.

Maya closed her eyes and trembled with anger, outraged at the injustice done to this girl. She'd promised Gina safety, an escape from the degradation and pain she'd endured, a chance at a normal life. And no one, not even Sanjeet Singh—a man whose power cowed police even beyond the Himalayas—had the right to drag her back.

"Leave," Gina murmured, her voice faint.

Maya snapped open her eyes. "Right. Let's go."

"No, you." The girl struggled to form her words. "Trap... Singh knows...who you are."

Maya went still. Singh knew she was the Leopard? How had he found out? Her identity was a carefully guarded secret, known only to a trusted few.

And if Singh had discovered the truth... Fear slithered

though her, a bone-deep feeling of dread. He must have infiltrated her inner group. It was the only explanation. Someone she trusted had betrayed her—which put dozens of lives at risk.

She shook her head to clear her mind. She'd worry about that problem later. Right now she had to focus on getting Gina to safety—before Singh or his henchmen came back.

But what about Deven? Would he try to stop them? She shot him a wary glance. He stood in the doorway, his eyes grim as he studied the girl, his large body blocking their path.

She didn't want to believe he was involved with Singh. Everything she'd ever known about him rebelled at the thought. He'd once shared her dreams, her plans. He'd been an avenger, a crusader for the downtrodden—or so she'd thought.

But even the most upstanding men were capable of horrendous cruelty, as she well knew.

Then his gaze collided with hers, and the turmoil in his eyes stole her breath. He was innocent. He had to be innocent. But then why was he here?

Before she could ask, he turned his head. "Lock the door and get out," he ordered. He stepped back into the other room and closed the door.

And then she heard voices. Deep, male voices. *Singh's men.*

She leaped up and lunged for the door, latching it with shaking hands. Then she whirled around and scanned the room, searching for a way to escape. Her gaze landed on the balcony doors. They were one story up, but it was their only hope.

She raced back to Gina, grateful the girl was alert. But Gina was weak, her thin body racked by fever—and that locked door wouldn't gain them much time.

"Gina, come on." She tugged the girl to her feet, keeping

her arm around her waist to support her, and hurried to the balcony across the room. Then she opened the doors and stepped out.

The night had cooled, and the air was heavy with the honeyed scent of orchids, moist from the recent monsoons. She peered into the darkness below the balcony as a truck engine rumbled to life. The servants' entrance was just around the corner. The commotion surrounding the catering trucks would help distract the guards.

But Gina was trembling violently, her teeth chattering, in no condition to climb to the ground. No wonder Singh had left her unguarded. He probably doubted she had the strength to escape.

Time to prove him wrong.

Maya quickly unwrapped her sari, shivering in her skirtlike petticoat and midriff-baring top. She looped the long strip of silk around the railing, then handed Gina one end of the cloth.

"All right, listen," she said, keeping her voice low. "We don't have much time. Climb over the railing and sit on the edge of the balcony." She pointed to the stones just beyond the rails. "Just hang on to the cloth. When I tell you to go, push off. That's all you have to do. Just hold on, and I'll lower you to the ground."

Assuming the fabric held.

Pushing aside that worry, she motioned toward the servants' entrance below. "The gate's right around the corner. Don't wait for me. As soon as you get to the ground, run. I'll meet you back at the shelter." She paused. "You understand?"

Gina nodded, and Maya gave her a hug, impressed that even in her weakened state, the girl had the spirit to fight.

She would need it to survive.

Maya helped her over the railing, watching nervously as she perched on the ledge.

"Okay, hold on." Her stomach tensing, Maya sat on the balcony floor and braced her feet on the rails. Then she adjusted her hold on the cloth and leaned back.

Voices rose outside the bedroom door. A heavy thud rattled the wood. Gina's gaze flew to hers, and Maya's own anxiety swelled. "Go!"

The girl jumped. The cloth went tight, nearly leaping from Maya's hands. She tightened her grip and held on.

But it wasn't easy. Pain bolted down her back like the sizzle of lightning. Her shoulders knotted and throbbed. She loosened her hold, trying to let the fabric out slowly so Gina wouldn't plunge to the ground—but the cloth tore through her palms. *Too fast.*

She fought to keep it steady. Sweat dripped in her eyes and stung. Her arms ached; her entire body shuddered with pain as she wrenched the cloth back and held on.

Again. Her palms burning, she inched out the fabric. Her thigh muscles bunched from the strain. The long cloth jerked along the railing, inch by agonizing inch, still too far from the ground.

And then it stopped. Panting, Maya played out the fabric. The rails bit into her feet. But the darned cloth still didn't move.

Suddenly it ripped, went slack, rocking her back against the stone floor. Below her, Gina let out a startled cry.

Horrified, Maya pushed herself to her knees and peered through the railing, fear like a vise on her throat. But Gina got to her feet, staggered into the shadows and disappeared into the night.

She'd made it.

Maya slumped against the railing and pressed her hand to

her racing heart. Feverish or not, Gina was a survivor. She'd get past the gate, make her way through the ancient city of Kintalabad's warren of streets to the shelter, where she'd be safe.

But now Maya had to get herself down. Her arm muscles cramping, sharp spasms racking her thighs, she pulled herself to her feet.

Another thump sounded behind her. The bedroom door burst open, and she spun around. Singh's men rushed in, their weapons drawn.

Her luck had just run out.

Chapter 2

Maya had gone insane. Breaking into Singh's palace was foolhardy, suicidal. She had to be out of her mind.

Deven Kapur charged after Singh's men through the doorway, his 9 mm Ruger drawn, his fear for her out of control. He'd tried to buy her time, tried like hell to delay Singh's guards so she and the kid could escape.

He just hoped it had been enough.

Dreading what would happen if they hadn't escaped, he skidded to a stop behind the guards. He scanned the empty bedroom, glanced over their heads to the balcony doors.

His hopes tanked.

The kid was gone, but Maya still stood with her back to the railing, defiantly facing the men. Her dark eyes were fierce with bravado, her chin raised to a challenging tilt. But her lush body quivered, and she'd closed one hand over the medallion she always wore around her neck, a gesture he knew betrayed her fear.

She should be afraid—because no way would these thugs resist her. She was a far too beautiful prize. The low light shimmered on her exotic cheekbones, caressed the full, ripe swell of her lips. A tiny diamond beckoned from one delicate nostril, and her thick, black braid swept past her hips.

She'd removed the outer part of her sari, and her short, tight top displayed her breasts to perfection, exposing the seductive slope of her waist. She was a fantasy, built like a Hindu goddess, all soft, sensual curves and satin skin.

No, these guards would never resist her. And if Singh got his hands on her...

Not an option.

Deven locked his jaw and bared his teeth. He tightened his grip on the gun. He'd left Romanistan twelve years ago to keep this woman safe. He'd be damned if he'd let Singh harm her now.

But he also had a mission to protect, a cover to maintain—which meant he couldn't tip off the guards.

"It's her, all right," one of the guards—a squat, bulldog of a man with powerful forearms—said. "She's got the medallion Singh wants."

Medallion? Singh wanted Maya's good luck charm? Deven frowned, wondering how that fit into his case, but quickly shook off the thought. He couldn't get distracted. He had to focus, get her out of the line of fire while he took down the guards.

But the other, wiry guard stepped closer to Maya. "Where's the girl?" he demanded. "Where did she go?"

Maya angled her head and leaned back against the railing, drawing the men's eyes to her breasts. "I only did what Deven told me," she said, her voice a sultry purr. "He said if I got rid of the girl, we'd be alone." She met his eyes, affected a pout. "You didn't say you were bringing friends, Dev."

His gut went cold. Did she have any idea what she'd just done? She'd used his real name and demolished his cover, put both their lives on the line.

He couldn't avoid a bloodbath now.

The two guards swiveled to face him.

Maya tumbled over the railing, then jumped.

Deven fired, taking out the heavyset guard closest to the balcony, but a sudden heat blazed through his arm as a bullet struck home. *Damn!* He lunged back into the adjoining room and kicked the door shut, lurched toward the adjacent balcony doors.

The door crashed open behind him. He spun back and squeezed off a round to pin down the remaining guard. He yanked open the balcony doors and raced to the railing, then vaulted the barrier and leaped.

He landed ten feet below the balcony in a patch of mud. The impact jolted his legs and knocked his breath loose, but he rolled, paratrooper style, and gained his feet. His momentum pushed him into a run.

He sprinted through the unlit garden, trying to see where Maya had gone. But a burst of semiautomatic gunfire crackled above him. He zigzagged, his pulse hammering, dodging bushes and trees. He reached the end of the building, flattened himself deeper into the shadows against the wall.

His breath sawed. His triceps muscle burned. He ignored his injured arm, ejected the spent magazine from the Ruger, and rammed another in place. The gunfire would have alerted the security guards. They would close down the compound, turn on the spotlights. He had to find Maya fast.

A shadow moved at the edge of his vision. He raised his gun, took aim at the running figure, but the graceful gait halted his fire. *Maya.* Gunfire tatted at her from the nearby guardhouse. He leaped out in a rush of adrenaline, shot back to distract the guards.

Then he went after Maya. His head down, he raced toward a truck parked near the gate. Lead thudded into the ground around him, spraying mud over his feet. He reached the truck, dove for cover, then crouched and heaved for air.

Sweat streamed down his cheeks. The harsh smell of gunfire stung his nose. Where was she? He squinted at the shadows, refusing to let her escape. That woman owed him some answers: who the girl was. Why Singh cared about her good luck charm. What she knew about Singh's plans.

He peeked out from behind the truck and fired at the guardhouse. A shadow darted through the gate.

Now.

His energy surging, he ran to the gate in a barrage of gunfire. He slipped through, his eyes on Maya, and ducked behind a car parked outside the wall. She disappeared into a narrow street nearby.

Deven waited, listening intently. Echoes of gunshots rang in his ears. Shouts came from the compound, drowning out the strains of a musician's horn.

He started to rise, but bullets whined past, pinning him down. He waited a beat, then dove toward a Tata SUV. He twisted beneath it, crawled on his belly to the opposite side. Then, keeping his head low, he sprinted away from the car.

He spotted Maya down the block—a dark form racing through the night. Determined to keep her in sight, he followed, his feet pounding the stones. When he reached the corner, he slowed.

He flattened himself against the brick building, ignoring the raw fire burning his arm. Breathing hard, he peered around the corner, saw her scurry around a pile of garbage. A stray dog yipped as she passed.

More relaxed now, he waited until she rounded the block, letting her lengthen her lead. Then he followed more slowly, keeping a safe distance behind. She glanced back, and he stepped in a doorway. She ran flat out, and he resumed the chase.

But as he trailed her through the maze of ancient streets, his admiration grew. He'd forgotten how quick she was, how stealthy. She slipped through the shadows like a pro, proof of a childhood spent surviving these streets.

But he had survived them, too. And they were in a neighborhood he knew well, the oldest part of Kintalabad—a chaotic tangle of narrow streets where he'd spent the three best years of his life.

His years with Maya.

He shoved that thought from his mind, unwilling to dwell on the past. He had to focus on salvaging his mission—and keeping Maya in sight.

She cut through another alley, and pavement gave way to mud. Low doorways dotted the sagging wooden buildings. A jumble of electrical wires dipped to the ground. Pallets lay scattered across the narrow lane, along with trampled debris from a daytime bazaar.

Maya kept jogging, hurrying past apartments draped with ropes of garlic to a long industrial building with a metal door. He followed as close as he dared, then hid in a recessed doorway to watch.

She glanced around at the alley, then fumbled with the drawstring of her sari and untied a key. She unlocked the door, stepped inside.

He leaped out and hurtled the remaining distance, slamming his shoulder into the door. It crashed back against the frame.

Maya shrieked and spun to face him. He backed her against

the inside wall. He planted his hands beside her head, trapping her in place while the door behind them clicked shut.

Their ragged pants filled the silence. Light from a nearby lamp burnished her hair. "What do you want?" she demanded, her eyes flashing.

Good question. Vengeance. Justice.

Her.

He gazed down at her, his rapid breath dueling with hers. And for a moment he indulged himself, drinking in the vision of beauty before him—her creamy, pouting lips, her mesmerizing eyes, the feminine curve of her cheeks.

He inhaled, and her scent curled around him like a forbidden memory, that erotic scent he'd fought for years to forget. And images crowded inside him, raw, carnal memories that had been forever scorched in his nerves—her sultry kiss, her husky moans, the feel of her naked skin slick against his.

Desire shuddered through him, a deep, feral hunger he'd long suppressed. But he couldn't have her. He could never have her. He'd learned that twelve years back.

"Answers," he said, his voice too deep, too rough. "I want to know what's going on."

"As if you don't know."

"I wouldn't be here if I did."

She flinched back as if he'd struck her. Sudden pain haunted her eyes. But she lifted her chin, curled her lips in a show of scorn. "Right. How could I forget? You couldn't leave me fast enough, could you?"

He steeled his jaw against a rush of guilt, wishing that he could deny it. But he had acted badly. He'd left with no warning, no explanation. He'd experienced heaven in her arms, then disappeared.

But he hadn't been able to tell her the truth. He couldn't

take the risk. It had been safer to let her despise him, better that he irrevocably crushed every tie.

"I have nothing to say to you," she added, her dark eyes blazing. "Not now, not ever. So get out and leave me alone."

If only he could. He'd spent months cultivating his role, working his way through Singh's ranks, gaining access to his inner group—only to have her blow that cover to shreds.

Now he couldn't go back to Singh. But neither could he abandon his goal. Interpol was depending on him to ferret out Singh's plans.

And right now Maya was his only clue.

"Maya?" A woman's worried voice came from down the hall. "Are you all right?"

Tension still crackled between them. Maya's eyes stayed locked on his. But then she released her breath in a huff and turned her head. "I'm fine, Ruchi. Did Gina make it back all right?"

"Yes. I've got her in the kitchen. I gave her a sponge bath to bring down the fever, and I'm heating some broth for her now."

"Good. Try to get some aspirin down her. I'll be right there to help." Maya's gaze swiveled back to his. She frowned, as if weighing her options.

He didn't budge.

But his mind shuffled through impressions, working to make sense of it all. Singh ran an international export business headquartered in Kintalabad, the capital city of Romanistan, which served as a front for his smuggling pursuits—drugs, antiquities, illegal weapons. He used those profits to fund a number of terrorist groups. Interpol had hired Magnum, the private military company Deven worked for, to infiltrate Singh's organization and determine the extent of those terrorist ties.

One of Singh's most lucrative sidelines involved trafficking women to the brothels in India. But over the years an underground rescue operation had disrupted that business. And earlier that evening, Deven had caught wind of Singh's plan to lure the group's leader—a stealthy, nocturnal operator code-named the Leopard—into a trap.

That kidnapped girl had been the bait. Maya had rescued her. And Maya obviously ran some sort of shelter, judging by what he'd just heard.

The pieces clicked. His jaw turned slack. He stared at her in disbelief. "It's you. You're the Leopard."

She flushed, confirming his suspicions, and he made a sound of disgust. He should have guessed. She fit the Leopard's description exactly—determined, persistent, a champion of the downtrodden. Daring enough to take on a ruthless criminal like Sanjeet Singh.

She sighed again, more heavily this time, then shoved her palms against his chest. "Let me go. I'll tell you what I know, and then you can leave."

He waited a beat, making sure she knew she couldn't escape him, then stepped away from the wall. She tossed back her braid, straightened her skirt, and shot him a disgruntled look.

"In here." She turned and led him through the hallway into a lounge.

Still stunned by the revelation, wondering why he hadn't made the connection sooner, he ducked under the low doorway. He crossed a threadbare rug, passed a battered desk and mismatched chairs. The smell of steaming rice and dal drifted in from a nearby room, making his stomach growl.

She eyed his arm. "You're bleeding." Her words came out clipped, and he knew it cost her to be polite.

"I'll live." He lowered himself to a sagging sofa, glanced

at his sleeve saturated with blood. He'd deal with his injury later, after he found out what was going on.

She perched across from him in one of the armchairs, and he shifted his gaze to hers. And without warning, her beauty struck him again—her exotic eyes, the provocative fullness of her lips, the gleam of her tawny skin.

His body stirred, the reaction predictable. Maya had gotten to him since he was fifteen. But he refused to let the chemistry they'd always had knock his mind off course.

She crossed her arms, flattened her lips. "So what do you want to know?"

How she'd become the Leopard. Who her contacts were. What she knew about Singh. "Tell me what you do."

She shrugged. "We rescue the women Singh's smuggling through the mountains into the sex trade. We send other teams into India to bring back the ones we've missed. Once they're here, we either reunite them with their families, or train them and help them find jobs if their families won't take them back."

His eyes held hers. A spurt of admiration warmed his heart. "Just what you said you'd do."

"Yes." She raised a finely arched brow. "Some people keep their word."

His jaw tightened as the barb hit home. It shouldn't matter what she thought of him. She was safer if she believed the worst.

But damned if it still didn't hurt.

"So how did the girl end up at Singh's?" he asked.

Maya pulled her thick braid over her shoulder and twisted the ends. "She has malaria. I needed to get her to a doctor and I didn't want to wait until night. Singh's men caught us. I got away. She didn't."

She sighed and released her braid. The black strands nestled between her breasts, and he forced his gaze to her face.

On the surface, the story made sense. Singh didn't tolerate interference, and the Leopard had disrupted his business for years. And he never forgave a grudge, as Deven knew.

But Deven's instincts told him there was something else going on, another reason Singh had tried to capture her now. He stood, sending a gecko scurrying under the couch, and paced to a long bank of windows still darkened by night. His reflection frowned back in the glass.

He'd spent years studying Singh, learning how he worked, how he thought. And one thing he'd discovered about the man—he buried his secrets deep. Even infiltrating his inner group and searching the palace compound had yielded few new facts.

Except that Internet chatter was heating up. Singh had started traveling more. And rumor had it he was planning something big, something deadly, something so catastrophic it had Interpol running scared.

Interpol was depending on Deven to find out what. The stability of the region, even the world, could be at stake—as well as his private plans for revenge.

Especially if, as Interpol feared, Singh had ties to the Order of the Black Crescent Moon—a fanatical terrorist organization intent on wiping out the Roma worldwide. Interpol suspected the group was plotting to overthrow Romanistan, the Roman's ancient homeland, which could spark a global war.

But Deven hadn't found proof of that. He'd hardly learned a thing in the past few months. Frustrated, he turned and met Maya's gaze. "I need to talk to the girl."

"Not until you tell me what you're doing with Singh."

"I can't. It's safer if you don't get involved," he added when she opened her mouth to protest.

"I'm already involved. He's targeting the women I've promised to protect."

And now she'd further defied Singh to rescue the girl—an act of rebellion the man would crush hard.

"Look," he said, trying to sound reasonable. "We don't have time to argue. I need to talk to the girl and find out what she knows. And you need to get out of here before Singh shows up. I don't think we were followed, but I can't be sure."

Her face paled. Fear moved into her eyes. "You're right. The girls…" She leaped up, ran into the kitchen. "Ruchi," she called. "Get the girls out fast."

He followed more slowly, then leaned against the doorjamb to watch. Maya rushed to the woman standing at an ancient stove and spoke in low, urgent tones. The woman's gaze flew to his and then she raced off.

Maya turned to the table where the kidnapped girl sat shivering in a pile of blankets. The kid's hair was wet, her thin face flushed. She looked scrawny, fragile and so damned young it made his gut roil.

One more reason to see Singh dead.

"Oh, Gina," Maya murmured. She dropped to her knees, enveloped the feverish kid in a hug.

The girl shot him a nervous look, so he averted his eyes, scanning the drab, industrial-sized kitchen instead. Dented pots steamed on the stove. Cracked dishes were piled high beside a tub. But a riot of red and purple flowers fractured the drabness—big bunches of them spilling from vases and jars along the counter, like defiant beacons of warmth and hope.

And despite the danger, despite the intense pain slashing his arm, the corner of his mouth ticked up. This place was exactly what Maya had always dreamed of. She was a born crusader, a one-person army against the world.

His gaze traced the slope of her back as she comforted the girl, the seductive flare of her hips. It wasn't just her beauty that had ensnared him back then, although her lush curves and fiery passion had kept him enthralled. But it was her zeal for justice, the relentless way she battled for the underdogs, that had thoroughly captured his heart.

She'd been his perfect match.

He released a sigh. But that was a lifetime ago—before Singh had caught up, before his mother had died.

Before he'd had to leave the woman he loved.

He pushed away from the wall and strode to the spigot, noting the first aid supplies nearby. "Mind if I use some gauze?"

"Go ahead. Do you need help?"

"No." He ran the tap, splashed water on his torn skin. It was only a graze, still bleeding, but nothing he couldn't survive. He grabbed a dishrag, blotted his skin dry, and turned back to the kidnapped girl. "But I do need information. What did you hear while you were at Singh's?"

The girl jumped at the sound of his voice, then shrank behind Maya to hide. "He's all right. He won't hurt you," Maya said, her tone soothing. But the girl cowered and shook her head.

Deven tamped down his impatience with effort. He understood the kid's fear. He'd grown up on the run as well, always wary, always careful to protect himself. But he didn't have time to coax her to talk.

He wrapped his arm with the gauze, then retreated to the doorway, hoping the space would help her relax.

"He wanted you," the girl said to Maya, her voice so weak Deven had to strain to hear. "Your good luck charm... He said...to get it."

Maya tossed him a glance. "It's how my people identify me."

Deven nodded. The guard had mentioned her medallion. And it made sense that Singh would want it; he could use it to reel in Maya's people and destroy the network that had plagued him for years.

But why now? Why bother taking down Maya's organization when he had something more sinister planned? The timing of this felt all wrong.

Deven shifted, a restless feeling churning inside—the feeling that he was missing something. Something important.

He straightened and strode back to the counter, his disquiet building with every step. He'd spent months hunting for clues—searching Singh's palace, conducting surveillance, discreetly questioning guards. He'd even managed to hack into Singh's computer. But examining his files had yielded little new information, except for Singh's offbeat interest in Himalayan history and language.

Certainly nothing related to Maya's medallion.

Unless… He stopped, turned. His gaze sharpened on the charm nestled against her chest. And suddenly, a memory bubbled up, an image he'd suppressed for years—a hot, sweltering night, insects buzzing in the darkness, the musky scent of sex in the air. Maya lying in his arms, surrounded by candles, the low light making the heavy, silver medallion she wore around her neck gleam.

The medallion with a Hindu goddess on one side, a strange inscription on the back—astrological symbols, exotic writing.

Ancient writing?

His pulse picked up. His gaze narrowed on the medallion still glinting against her smooth skin. And a sudden thought occurred to him. What if Singh was searching for the Roma crown, the last of the three medieval treasures? What if that medallion was some sort of clue? It would explain Singh's interest and provide a link to the Order of the Black Crescent Moon, which believed the Roma stole the treasures from them.

Of course, he could be jumping to conclusions. Singh's interest was hardly unique; ever since the first of those treasures had surfaced in Spain several months back, every historian, antiquity collector and treasure seeker the world over had begun hunting for the other two.

Or Singh might only want the medallion for the obvious reason—to flush out Maya's group. The inscription could be meaningless—a tradesman's mark, a forgotten prayer— nothing of interest to Singh.

But Deven didn't believe in coincidence. And he never ignored his instincts.

And right now his instincts told him that whatever Singh had planned, that medallion was involved.

Maya's eyes narrowed on his. Her hand closed around the medallion's chain, as if she could read his mind. "Gina, go get dressed," she told the girl, but her eyes didn't waver from his. "We need to leave fast." The girl staggered to her feet and scurried away.

He kept his tone casual. "Where are you going?"

"I've got places."

"I'll go with you."

"Forget it. I don't need your help."

She never had—or so she'd thought. But he wasn't letting her—or that medallion—out of his sight.

"You can tell me more about Singh as we go," he said.

She shook her head, and her long braid swept her hips. "I've already told you what I know. There's no point hanging around. Now I need to go." She turned, headed toward the same door the rescued girl had used.

But he crossed the kitchen in a few long strides, beating her to the door, then slapped his palm on the frame to keep it closed.

She wheeled around and raised her brows. "Do you mind? You said there isn't much time."

"I also said I'm going with you." Still blocking the door, he leaned close—close enough to see the deep flush darken her face, the sudden anger spark in her eyes.

Close enough to feel the seductive warmth of her skin. His pulse picked up speed. He lowered his gaze to her lips—her smooth, moist lips—then over the graceful slope of her neck. And he was intensely, vibrantly aware of how close she was, that with one small move he could taste her mouth, her heat, and relive the pleasure he'd denied himself for years.

But he had no business touching Maya. She could never be his. He forced his gaze back up. "Just until you're safe," he added. And he got that medallion from her.

Her delicate nostrils flared. Skepticism mingled with the anger in her eyes. She didn't trust him.

Smart woman.

But then she shrugged. "Fine. Do whatever you want. I'll be right back."

He wasn't fooled. "You've got three minutes. Then I'm coming in."

He held her gaze a heartbeat longer, then stepped back to let her pass. She jerked the door open, marched from the kitchen into the hall. The door slammed shut behind her.

And the irony struck him. He'd spent twelve years trying to forget this woman. Twelve years yearning for her, aching for her, suffering for her. But for her safety, he'd had to stay as far from her as he could.

Now for the same reason, he couldn't let her out of his sight.

And he didn't know which was worse.

Chapter 3

As soon as the door clicked shut behind her, Maya bolted down the deserted hallway past the shelter's bedrooms—their bunk beds empty, their doors now hanging ajar. She skidded into her own room and kicked off her sandals, filled with the urgent need to flee.

She had to get rid of Deven. She knew that he planned to stick with her; she'd recognized the obstinate set of his mouth. But she'd spent her entire life on her own and refused to depend on him now.

She also didn't trust him—and not only because of their past. He'd evaded her questions, never explained why he was with Singh. And she had too much at risk to take a chance.

Working quickly, she snatched a T-shirt from her closet, then pulled her jeans from her dresser drawer just as Ruchi popped into her room. "Everyone's gone," Ruchi told her. "I sent them to Leena."

"Good." Leena ran another station on their underground

network, and Maya could trust her to keep the girls safe. She glanced at the door to make sure Deven hadn't followed, then peeled off the rest of her clothes. "What about Gina?"

"I told Leena how sick she is. She's calling a doctor now."

"Thanks." She just hoped help didn't come too late. "You'd better go," she added.

"What about you?"

"I'll catch up." She tugged on her jeans, yanked the T-shirt over her head and pulled on her canvas shoes. There was no time to bother with socks.

She glanced at Ruchi, who hadn't moved, and her feeling of urgency grew. Ruchi was the first woman Maya had rescued and her best friend. But no matter how close they were, she couldn't endanger her, too.

"Go on," she told her. "I'll meet you later. It's safer if we split up."

"I guess." Ruchi hesitated and gnawed her lip. "But what about the man in the kitchen?"

Excellent question. Grimacing, Maya grabbed a small day pack from her desk and stuffed in some extra clothes. "Tell him I'll be right there."

"But—"

"I'll explain it all later, okay? Just go."

"All right." Ruchi moved to the door and looked back. "But be careful." She turned and hurried away.

Knowing Deven wouldn't stay put long, Maya hauled a straight-backed chair to the window and climbed onto the sill. Then she swung her legs out the window and jumped.

She landed in the mud with a muffled thump. Her heart racing, she moved away from the light pooling from her bedroom, her feet crunching on broken glass. Then she paused by the edge of the building, slung the backpack over her shoulder, and waited for her eyes to adjust to the night.

The cool, dark air prickled the skin on her forearms. The scent of moist earth teased her lungs. Trying not to think about the man she'd left prowling around her kitchen, she sucked in a deep, slow breath to steady her nerves.

But the alley behind the shelter was quiet—too quiet. No stray dogs howled. No people stirred. Not even a cricket chirped.

She stood motionless, her senses alert, her nerves stretched tight at the lack of sound. The night air pulsed with the deepening hush, filling her with a sudden unease.

Something was wrong.

Then a shadow in her peripheral vision moved. A slight crunch exploded near her ear. She wheeled around, then went dead still as the barrel of a gun pressed under her chin.

"That's right. Don't move," a man's harsh voice grated in her ear.

Her throat closed up. Cold sweat trickled down her scalp. He stepped closer, thrusting his dark face inches from hers. The stench of unwashed flesh made her stomach rebel.

"Now hand it over," he demanded. "Nice and slow. No fast moves or I'll shoot."

The gun dug deeper into her neck. A wild sound stuck in her throat. She fisted her trembling hands, refusing to let her voice shake, forcing the words from her mouth. "Hand over what?"

"Don't play dumb. The medallion. Now give it to me fast."

The medallion? She blinked, trying to make sense of the weird demand. Singh must have sent him. He must want to use the medallion to find—and kill—her helpers. She darted her gaze over the shadows, knowing she had to protect them at any cost.

"All right," she said, hoping he didn't notice the chain around her neck. "I'll get it. It's in my pack. I just need a little space."

Moving slowly, warily, she reached for the strap on her backpack. The man eased back his weapon, just as she'd hoped. She hauled in a breath for courage, prepared to fling the pack at his face.

But a huge form lunged from the shadows. She dove, hit the mud, rolled frantically to get out of the line of fire. A gunshot blasted the air.

He'd missed. She regained her feet in a burst of adrenaline, her ears ringing from the deafening roar. Knowing every second counted, she seized her bag and ran.

Her feet pounded the mud as she raced down the alley. Dark buildings flew past in a blur. She turned the corner, her breath sawing, then fled down another dirt road.

She picked up speed and skirted a trash pile. Sheer urgency screeched through her nerves. She had to get away, hide. She couldn't let the gunman catch up.

But someone grabbed her arm, whipped her around.

Deven. She stumbled back, stunned by his lethal speed. But he didn't give her time to catch her breath. He caught her arm again, yanked her into motion and hauled her down the street.

She tripped, but he pulled her upright. She jerked back, but he didn't slow. Incensed at his high-handed manner, she tried to wrench her arm free, but he just towed her down the alley, his footsteps slamming the ground. She had to jog to keep up with his strides.

He turned at the end of a building. His fingers bit into her arm. Fed up with being shoved around, she pulled back and dug in her heels. He stopped and spun her around.

Even in the dim light she could see his eyes burn. His scar formed an angry slash. And fury vibrated off him in waves, sparking the air like an electric charge.

Realizing he'd reached the flash point, she backed up, bumped into the building's wall.

"Are you out of your bloody mind?" he raged, stepping toward her. "Don't you ever do that again. *Ever.* Do you hear me?" He grabbed her shoulders, holding her captive. She grunted and clenched her teeth.

"Let me go," she gritted out. She tried to shake his hands off, but he tightened his grip even more.

"Do you have any idea how close that was?" His deep voice trembled with outrage. His dark eyes drilled into hers. "You nearly died back there."

"I know that." She shoved his chest, but he didn't move. His furious face glowered at hers.

"The hell you do. You have no idea what you're up against. Do you think this is some kind of game?"

"Game?" Her face grew hot at the accusation, and her indignation soared. "Who are you to barge in after all these years and accuse me of playing games? I know exactly what I'm up against. I've seen the girls Singh's kidnapped and locked in cages, the despicable acts he's forced them to do. Children—poor, innocent children—whose only crime was walking to the market, or trusting the wrong adult."

And now she'd failed them, too.

Guilt shuddered through her, halting her tirade—guilt that she'd let them down. Guilt that she'd caused them more fear. Guilt that she'd brought danger back into their lives, terrible danger, after she'd promised them they'd be safe.

But she couldn't dwell on that now. She had troubles of her own to solve, including escaping this furious man.

She wrenched herself loose from Deven's grasp and lifted her chin. "So don't tell me about Singh. I know more about him than you do."

"Don't be so sure."

The stark tone of his voice knocked her off stride. She paused, her temper abruptly deflated, struck by the bleakness she heard. But before she could question what it meant, he shifted away.

"Look, Maya." He gripped the back of his neck, and the white gauze around his biceps gleamed. "I'm not kidding about the danger. You defied Singh and hurt his business. You broke into his palace and took that girl. He's not going to let that go."

"I know." She had to run, far from the girls she was trying to help, far from anyone and any place she knew. Because Deven was right. Singh wouldn't give up. He'd stop at nothing to get her—or her medallion, it seemed.

Swallowing hard to quell her fear, she thought back on the gunman's words. "Why is Singh so obsessed with my medallion?"

"Interesting question." His gaze sharpened. "What do you know about it?"

"Nothing. It's just a good luck charm." One of thousands like it sold in tourist shops throughout the Himalayas. On the front was the Hindu goddess Parvati, consort of Shiva. On the back were some astrological symbols and a worn-out inscription she couldn't read. It was old, possibly an antique, but hardly valuable.

Except to her.

She didn't know where it came from. She only knew that she'd always had it, from her earliest memories on. And it had become a symbol to her, a sign that whoever gave it to her—even if only a passing stranger—had cared enough to wish her luck.

Which had meant the world to an orphaned child.

But that didn't explain Singh's interest. She met Deven's steady gaze. "Why do you think he wants it?"

"To trap your people, take down your network, I'd guess."

"That's what I figured." But the unwavering way Deven watched her made her uneasy. She studied his hard face darkened by shadows, the piercing look in his eyes.

And a sudden awareness slithered through her, like a shiver crawling under her skin. Something else was going on here. Something ominous.

A deep chill seeped through her bones.

"But you think there's another reason," she said slowly.

"I don't know."

Was that true? She studied his cryptic eyes, the unyielding line of his mouth. She'd been able to read him once. As a teenager, she'd spent hours memorizing the sexy way his lips quirked, the crinkles that fanned his eyes when he smiled. She'd learned how his forehead creased, how those dark eyes flickered with anger, how his face turned taut with desire.

But he was a stranger now. A man with secrets. A man she didn't dare trust.

She slid her gaze to the handgun nestled in the waistband of his jeans, then back to that jagged scar. He'd grown even more dangerous since their school days. She'd be a fool to let down her guard.

"I only know that Singh wants it," he said, his voice even. "And you'll be safer if you give it to me."

"What?"

"You heard me."

"Forget it. I'm not giving any medallion to you."

"Maya, be reasonable. It's only a good luck charm. It's not worth your life."

But Singh thought it was. And Deven had been at Singh's… A sudden suspicion flared. "So that's why you're here. You want my medallion, too."

His mouth flattened. "I'm here because I'm trying to keep you safe."

"Right. And I'm Mother Teresa." She ignored his deepening scowl. "Listen, Deven. I don't need your protection, and I don't want it. I've gotten along fine without you for years. And you can forget about the medallion. I'm not giving it up."

"Think again."

He leaned toward her. She bumped back against the brick wall. He braced his hands on either side of her head, trapping her with his big body. The move was threatening, intimate.

Wayward thrills rushed over her skin.

"Give me the medallion, Maya."

Her pulse raced at his husky tone. Her disloyal heart tumbled hard. "What good will that do? Singh's already after me."

"But I can distract him, buy you time. Give you a chance to escape."

The heat from his body made it hard to think. His masculinity quickened her blood. She struggled to hold on to her anger, her suspicions. After all, she'd come across Deven at Singh's!

But he was so close, so male. She shook her head, fighting to ignore her traitorous instinct, to forget the exciting pleasure they'd shared. "It won't make any difference who has the medallion. You said it yourself. I've been hurting his business, defying him for years. Even if I get away now, he's not going to give up."

He didn't answer, but his mouth tightened. His eyes turned grimmer yet. And she knew he couldn't argue with that. Singh would never leave her alone.

"Then there's only one option." The words sounded dragged from his mouth. "You'll have to stay with me."

"Forget it."

"That wasn't a request." His dark gaze kept her pinned. His big body locked her in place. And she remembered how easily he'd tackled her at the palace, how expertly he'd trailed her through the streets. How he'd anticipated that she would try to escape him—and caught up to her again.

So running from him would be pointless. But she didn't want him around. The one time she'd let down her guard and allowed him into her life he'd promised her marriage, love… and then fled.

But she also had to be practical. Singh's criminal organization ran the city of Kintalabad, and his power extended farther than that—throughout Romanistan, throughout the entire Himalayan region, even to other parts of the world. And it was one thing to thwart his smuggling operations. She knew his routes, who to bribe. But this… She had no idea what was going on here, or why her medallion mattered. How could she fight an unknown?

And she had no one else to turn to. She couldn't ask her friends for help; she would only endanger them more.

She studied the deep grooves bracketing Deven's mouth, the determined look in his eyes. She didn't have much choice. She had to trust him.

She just prayed she wasn't making a mistake.

"All right. We'll stick together. But just until we find out why Singh wants the medallion, and then I'm gone."

"Promise me," he demanded. "I want your word. No climbing out windows, no jumping off balconies. You try to escape me one more time, and I'll rip that thing off your neck."

"I said I'd work with you." Her frustration rose. "What do you want me to do? Sign a contract in blood?"

Tension throbbed between them. His dark eyes smoldered on hers. "No," he said, his voice turning gravelly. "It's not your blood I want."

His eyes dropped to her mouth.

Her heart lost its beat.

He wouldn't dare.

Her pulse picked up speed. Sudden heat pooled in her blood. Her body tightened, the thought of his lips on hers rooting her in place.

His big hand clamped her jaw. His callused thumb brushed her throat, making tingles chase over her skin.

And that ticked her off. She was through with this man, through with his lies. She might be forced to work with him, but no way would she let him—or her hormones—take charge.

With effort, she shook off the lust. "I've got two conditions of my own, though."

His eyes narrowed, and he cocked his head. "Which are?"

"I want to know what you're doing with Singh."

"And the other?"

"The medallion stays with me. It's my medallion, my past. If it means anything, I deserve to know."

His gaze stayed on hers. For an eternity, he didn't move. But then he nodded. "Agreed." He lowered his hand and paused, and that bleak look returned to his eyes. "But be careful, Maya. Sometimes the past holds secrets. And you might not like what you find."

He stepped back into the darkness, his face again shrouded

by night. And she slumped against the wall—shaken by his words, the desire that heated her blood, that tortured look in his eyes.

What had he meant? Had he learned something bad about his past? Was there more to him than she knew?

She closed her fingers around her medallion, battling back a sudden swell of sympathy, annoyed by the effort it took—because no matter how appealing he was, no matter what memories he evoked, she didn't dare trust him again. Not completely.

He was too secretive, too dangerous.

For all she knew, *he* could be her enemy.

She straightened, cast him a wary gaze. Enemy or not, she had to keep him close.

But she would also protect her heart.

Chapter 4

Fate had one hell of a sense of humor.

Deven sat beside Maya just off the main square in the oldest part of Kintalabad hours later, still shaking his head in disbelief. It was bad enough to have his cover blown, his mission at risk and Singh in full pursuit. But being around Maya was worse, dredging up memories, stirring up long-buried yearnings he had no right to feel.

He braved a glance at her resting on the brick step beside him. The rising sun made her black hair gleam and cast her skin in a golden glow. His gaze lingered on the feminine arch of her cheekbones, the intriguing slope of her nose. She had a natural elegance, a mesmerizing sensuality that tugged at him deep in the gut.

Struggling to corral his thoughts, he shoved his hand through his uncombed hair. He was trapped in a cosmic joke, all right, forced to protect the one woman he'd sworn to avoid.

But he'd deal with it. He had no choice. Whether Maya wanted to admit it or not, she needed his help to survive.

And he needed that medallion.

So did Singh. His face hardening at the thought of Singh, Deven carefully studied the square for signs of his men. Women swept off the bricks with their handmade brooms. Farmers set up scales and unloaded potatoes and beans. In the distance drums beat and bells rang along with the chanting of morning prayers.

Just a typical morning in Kintalabad as the ancient city lumbered to life. But the peaceful scene didn't fool him. Singh had an extensive organization, with even the police at his disposal, thanks to the government officials he bankrolled. His men would be combing the city by now—questioning merchants, checking the alleys, posting roadblocks on the outlying roads. Deven needed to hurry, find out what that inscription meant and then hustle Maya out of town.

"You never said what you were doing at Singh's," she said, and he turned his attention to her. The soft light revealed the dark smudges shadowing her eyes, the exhaustion etched on her face. After the long hours they'd spent trekking through the city, he wished he could let her rest, but they didn't have the luxury of time.

"I told you before. I can't answer that."

"Can't? Or won't?"

"Both," he admitted. "It's too dangerous."

"I don't see why. If Singh catches me, it won't matter how much I know."

Not to her. Singh would never let her survive. But they had more than their own lives at stake.

Still, he'd promised her an explanation, and she was far too persistent to let it drop. He rubbed his unshaven jaw and debated how much to say. He finally opted for an abbreviated version of the truth.

"I work for a private military company."

Her eyebrows gathered. "What's that?"

"We provide bodyguards and equipment—armed reconnaissance planes, helicopter gunships to individuals and companies, even governments sometimes. Basically we're soldiers for hire."

"You mean you're a mercenary?" She sounded shocked.

"Something like that." He shrugged. "Interpol hired my company to investigate Singh. They needed someone to infiltrate his group, to do undercover work, and since I'm from Romanistan, I was the obvious choice."

"I see." Her frown deepened. Her gaze shifted to the plaza, then back. "What are you hoping to find?"

"I'm not sure."

"You must have some idea or they wouldn't have sent you in there."

She was right, but it was safer not to say. "I'll tell you this much. We know Singh has connections to various terrorist groups. He funnels them money and provides them with arms. We've also learned that he's planning something big, something dangerous."

"Like what?"

"That's what I'm trying to find out. This region's too volatile to ignore the threat." Besides the country's nuclear arsenal, the recently discovered oil deposits made Romanistan a coveted prize. And with the royal family in exile, and the leading political parties in chaos, a powerful thug like Singh could stage a coup—especially if he had a deranged terrorist group on his side.

"And you think my medallion has to do with this plan?"

"It might."

"But how could it?"

"I don't know." He spread his hands, unwilling to give her more details. The less she knew, the safer she'd be. "Look. I don't have proof, just a feeling. I could be wrong. But this is the only lead I have right now, and I need to check it out. You really don't know what that inscription means?"

"No." She drew her knees to her chest and hugged her legs. Her long braid slid over her back. "I showed it to a few people when I was younger, but no one knew what it was. I didn't bother to ask after that. It didn't seem important."

Not important? The irony made his mouth twist. If he was right, that medallion could determine the fate of countless innocent lives.

Of course, the medallion was a long shot. It might have nothing to do with the legendary crown or the Order of the Black Crescent Moon. Still, given the Internet chatter they'd heard…

She cut her gaze to his. "So what's your plan?"

"Find an Internet café, check online, see if anything comes up." He also needed to e-mail his Interpol contact and report that his cover was blown. "Singh has an interest in ancient languages. There might be a connection to your medallion."

"You think it's that old?"

"I think we need to find out."

She pursed her lips, fingered the chain around her neck. "Why don't we ask at an antique store? A dealer might know what it is."

"Too risky. Singh will be on the lookout for the medallion."

"We could draw the inscription. We don't have to say where we saw it."

He mulled that over. They needed to stay out of sight, not

traipse through shops drawing attention to themselves. But if they could get a lead…

"All right." They'd take the chance. He just hoped they wouldn't regret it. "We'll need paper, though."

"I'll get some." She started to stand, but he snagged her wrist, waiting until her gaze returned to his.

"Remember our agreement. No running off."

Her cheeks flushed. Sudden temper darkened her eyes. "I keep my promises, Deven."

Unlike him, she meant.

His face turned hot. He worked his jaw, forcing himself to hold her gaze while her eyes burned angrier yet. Then he nodded and released her wrist. She snatched it away and stalked off, her full hips swiveling, temper quickening her strides.

He let out a curse and massaged the dull ache pulsing between his brows. He didn't blame her for being angry. She had every right to despise him.

He wished he could tell her the truth and explain what had happened that night. How Singh had caught up. How Deven had seen his mother die. How Singh had murdered his former mistress for daring to escape his control—and stealing his most valuable prize.

How Deven had realized that Singh would continue to pursue him, that Singh would destroy everyone Deven knew until he surrendered to him, and that the only way he could keep Maya safe was to leave—and forever stay away.

He'd lost everything that night—his family, his identity, the woman he'd loved… And he'd hungered for her, suffered for her, year after miserable year. It had destroyed him to let her go.

But he'd had no choice. He'd had to sever his ties with Maya quickly, permanently. He'd had to hurt her so badly that she'd refuse to try to find him, or even think of him again.

So he'd abandoned her, using her orphaned past against her, striking her most vulnerable spot. He'd betrayed her trust, her faith.

He exhaled again, fingered the scar Singh had given him that night—a reminder of all that he'd lost. And a deep sense of loneliness coursed through him, that same aching weariness he'd borne for years.

But there was no point explaining why he'd left her. The past was gone. He couldn't change it. And they could never have a future together. The more she despised him, the more dishonorable she believed he was, the better off they'd both be.

So he had to forget the past, forget the pain, just focus on keeping her safe—and bringing down Sanjeet Singh.

Determined to keep his mind on track, he pulled his attention back to the square. A cow meandered by. A street vendor set up a wok and began to deep-fry food. A group of porters trudged past, their sandals flapping, bags of rice piled high on their backs.

But then Maya strolled back into view, her full breasts swaying beneath her blue T-shirt, her faded jeans molding her thighs, and he knew that he was doomed.

Fate was mocking him, all right. It was going to be agony keeping this headstrong woman safe—especially from himself.

"I got the paper," she said, her voice still clipped. She sat down beside him, pulled her medallion free from her T-shirt and her thick braid slid over his arm.

He gritted his teeth, tried to ignore the silky caress. "Draw fast. We need to get out of here." Before he gave in to temptation, loosened that shining mass of silky hair and did something they both would regret.

"All right." She glanced at the medallion and began to sketch.

"And don't draw the whole thing."

Her head came up. "Why not?"

"In case Singh's men get the paper somehow. If they have the inscription, they won't need us alive."

A glimmer of fear moved into her eyes. But she nodded, continued to sketch and Deven again scanned the square. More vendors arrived, setting out incense, pottery, trinkets to sell to passing tourists as the sun popped over the Himalayas and the day began.

"Is this enough?" She held up the paper, and he slanted his head. She'd sketched the top of the inscription, capturing the wavy lines that resembled Sanskrit.

"Yeah, that's good. Let's go." While she looped the medallion around her neck, he stood, then reached out his hand to help her up.

She hesitated, her eyes on his. And despite her anger, despite his vow to keep his distance, that deep-seated awareness thrummed between them, that unceasing drum of desire.

His heart thudded hard. She grabbed his hand, and he pulled her up, conscious of the warmth of her satiny skin, the lush fullness of her lips, her pulse growing hectic under his thumb. Unable to resist, he tugged her closer, needing to taste her mouth, wanting to trace the line of her jaw with his tongue.

A dog barked. He blinked, jolted back to reality. Appalled at his unruly reaction, he dropped her hand. "You lead. I'll watch our backs."

"Right." Her face flushed. She turned on her heel and stalked off.

Disgusted with himself, unable to believe he'd lost control like that, he trailed her around the square. So they still had chemistry. It didn't matter. He had no business touching Maya, no right to act on the attraction between them. He could never be the man for her.

And he sure didn't need the distraction. Singh's men would show up soon. Being careless could get them both killed.

Forcing himself to focus on his surroundings, he followed her up the narrow lane crowded with rickshaws, past shrines decorated with brightly colored prayer flags. Goats brayed. People streamed past. The pungent scent of incense filled the air.

Maya reached an antique shop and stopped. "How's this?"

He peered through the dirty window, made out a rickety lamp hanging inside. Then he glanced up the noisy street again, and a sense of uneasiness prickled his spine. He didn't like this. His head warned him to get off the street and hide. But they needed a direction, something to go on if they hoped to defeat Singh. "All right."

Even more alert now, he stooped through the low doorway and followed her into the shop. He scanned the stacks of oriental rugs, the Tibetan screens blackened with age. A bearded man with a Nepali hat stood at a table, rummaging through a cardboard box.

"Namaste," Maya called in greeting, and the man looked up. "I wondered if you might help us. We're trying to find out what this is and thought that you might know." She walked over, handed him the paper with the sketch she'd drawn.

The man flicked on a nearby lamp, held the paper to the halo of light. "Where did you see this?"

Deven shot Maya a warning glance, and she nodded that she understood. "On an old oil lamp my uncle has."

The man stroked his long beard and studied the sketch.

"That's only part of it," she added. "The rest is worn down and hard to see."

"Sorry. I have no idea." He handed the paper back.

"Is it a signature?" Deven pressed, hoping for a clue. "Maybe the mark of the company that made it?"

"I don't know." The man fingered his beard again. "You could ask Mr. Verma, two streets over. He collects lamps. Or Mr. Advani. He runs a bookstore up the street. He might have seen it somewhere."

"Thank you," Maya said, and smiled. "We appreciate it." The man nodded and turned back to his box.

Frowning, Deven exited the antique shop. As he'd expected, they hadn't learned anything new. Worse, the shopkeeper could now identify them to Singh's men.

His apprehension mounting, he swept his gaze down the crowded street. The growing throng made it harder to spot a tail, but would also help shield them from view.

"So what do you think?" Maya asked when she joined him outside. "Should we try the bookstore?"

His instincts warned against it. The more people who saw them—or that drawing—the greater the risk. But they still needed something to go on. "Yeah, but then that's it. We have to get off the streets."

They found the bookstore tucked beside a wood-carver's shop at the end of the narrow lane. Deven followed Maya into a musty room crammed with bookcases. More books were stacked on the floor.

"Quite a collection," Maya said as he trailed her through the maze of bookcases to the desk. "Hello?" she called when no one emerged. "Is anyone here?"

She turned back to face him and shrugged. But then a man

shuffled out from the back, his brown face furrowed with wrinkles, his thin shoulders stooped with age.

"Mr. Advani?" Maya repeated her story and handed him the sketch. He set it on the counter, pulled a magnifying glass from a drawer and switched on a goosenecked lamp.

"Interesting," he said after a moment.

Deven's gaze sharpened. "Do you recognize it?"

"I'm not sure. I saw something once…" He hobbled to a glassed-in bookcase behind the counter, pulled a key from his pocket and unlocked the door. Then he ran a gnarled finger along the spines of the hardback books. "No, it's not here." He closed and locked the case. "I might have the book in the back, though."

"A book about what?" Maya asked.

"Dead languages."

Deven's heart skipped. Excitement coursed through his veins. But he kept his features blank, his voice carefully neutral. "You think that's some kind of writing?"

"Possibly."

"What was the language called?"

The bookseller shook his head. "I don't remember. And I could be wrong. My memory's not that good anymore."

But it was possible.

Which meant he was on the right track. The medallion could be a clue—and the connection he'd been looking for to the deadly Black Crescent group.

"What are you thinking?" Maya murmured.

Deven shook his head to postpone her questions and looked at the bookseller again. "Can you look for the book? Now? We don't have much time." He pulled some rupees from his pocket, slid them across the counter.

The man nodded, pocketed the money and picked up the

paper again. It shook in his palsied hands. "Give me an hour. I'll know by then."

Deven hesitated, reluctant to let the drawing out of his hands.

"I can stay here and help," Maya offered, apparently sensing his dilemma.

Tempted to let her, Deven glanced uneasily toward the door. It might be safer to keep her here, hidden from sight, while he e-mailed his boss at Magnum that his cover had been blown. But if he left her alone and Singh's men caught up...

He shook his head. He couldn't do it. He met the bookseller's eyes. "We'll be back in an hour."

But as he stepped outside into the busy street, his sense of disquiet grew. Singh's men should be scouring the city by now. Why hadn't he spotted them yet?

"What are you thinking?" Maya asked again when she joined him outside.

"We'll talk later. Is there a place with Internet access near here?"

"Just around the corner."

"Good. Let's go."

Keeping alert, he led the way around the corner, coming out on a teeming street. They plunged into the stream of pedestrians and threaded their way through the morning traffic, dodging mopeds and three-wheeled *tempos,* skirting vendors and construction debris. A jumble of voices merged with the roar of traffic and honking horns.

Sucking in a breath of exhaust fumes, Deven skipped his gaze through the crowds. Still no sign of Singh's men—but he knew their luck couldn't hold.

"Here it is," Maya called, and he stopped. The sign in the window was written in various languages, which meant the

Internet café catered to tourists, which was good—less chance that Singh would find them here.

He stepped inside, scanned the dozens of wooden library carrels crammed into the stuffy room. A handful of early risers pecked at computers—two bearded backpackers, a few European tourists—no one who'd pay attention to them.

Reassured, he nodded to the kid manning the front desk, then chose a computer near the rear exit, making sure he still had a view of the street. He squeezed into the booth and started the computer, while Maya dragged over another plastic stool.

She scooted close and her thigh bumped his. Her shoulder nudged his arm. Trying to ignore her scent, her curves, he fastened his gaze on the street and waited for his account to boot up. Buses and trucks rumbled past. Red-robed monks hurried by. He drummed his fingers on the table, then fired off one e-mail to the head of Interpol in Romanistan and another to Skinner, the head of Magnum, to let them know that his cover was shot.

That done, he exited the program and glanced at Maya. And he knew from the intent way she watched him that she was piecing together information, thinking over what she'd just seen.

Deciding whether or not he'd told her the truth.

She dropped her gaze to the old scar slashing his face, then quickly looked away. And that hollow feeling unfurled in his chest again, the same dull ache that had plagued him for years—loneliness, fury at Singh, resentment over all he'd lost.

He blocked it off. He couldn't go there. Some things in life couldn't be changed—who he was, the revenge he needed to take.

"I copied Singh's hard drive when I was in the palace," he said.

Her eyes swiveled back to his. "You have it with you?"

"No. I didn't have time to get it when I left." Thanks to her. "But when I was making the copy, I checked his browsing history. He's been researching ancient languages."

"Ancient languages?" A small line furrowed her brow. "So there might really be something about my medallion he wants to know?"

"That's what I'm guessing."

"But what? What could it mean?"

"That's what we need to find out. I thought we could check out some Web sites, see if anything jumps out at us, then see what the bookseller turns up."

She crinkled her forehead, as if processing that news. "All right, but let me do it. I can type faster."

And he could keep his eye on the street. He stood, pressed back against the wall to let her by. She started past him, but her backpack snagged on the stool. She stumbled, and he grabbed her waist to keep her from pitching over the desk.

"Thanks," she said, sounding breathless. She regained her balance and continued by, but her jeans-clad bottom brushed his groin. His reaction was swift, uncontrollable.

They both froze.

His fingers dug into her waist. His blood pounded in his veins. And he grappled with the urge to bury his face in her shiny hair, pull her warm, pliant body back against his—and relive the ecstasy he'd denied himself for years.

But she wasn't his anymore—no matter how badly he'd missed her, no matter how desperately he ached to relive her touch.

He swallowed, beating back the hunger with effort, and pried his fingers loose. She slid past him and dropped onto the stool. Moving stiffly, he lowered himself beside her, not daring to look her way.

"Anything specific I should look for?" Her voice sounded strained.

Still not trusting himself, he fastened his gaze on the screen. But he was far too conscious of her tempting heat, the alluring fragrance of her skin. "I don't remember the Web sites, but he was checking languages of the Himalayas."

"All right." Her fingers tapped on the keyboard. "No articles yet," she said, still sounding distracted. "Just links to textbooks." She scrolled through the links, typed in a modified search.

He inhaled again, staring at the screen like a zombie, willing the fierce need to ease. But he couldn't stop the barrage of unwanted images—Maya laughing with him, plotting with him, sitting beside him just like this—their hands clasped, their shoulders touching, smiling into each other's eyes.

He gave his head a sharp shake, fighting to dispel the memories. He'd been so damned idealistic back then, so sure he could save the world. He'd planned to fight injustice, battle corruption, rescue those weaker than himself. And Maya had been right there with him. She'd been his partner, his fellow crusader, his soul mate.

No other woman had filled the void since then. None had even come close. And he realized with sudden clarity that he missed that friendship, that soul-deep connection, far more than the riveting sex.

And it was the one thing he could never regain.

"Deven," she whispered, her voice oddly choked. "Look outside."

He snapped his gaze toward the storefront window. Two men lurked by the door.

Singh's guards.

He swore, grabbed her arm and pulled her under the desk. While he'd been moping about his lot in life, Singh's men had finally caught up.

"Out the back door," he urged her. "Go!"

Still cursing, he pulled out his gun, then crawled after her across the wooden floor. Maya reached the door, leaped up and yanked it open. A shot rang out, splintering the doorjamb near her head, and she lunged through the open door.

His adrenaline surging, Deven scrambled to his feet behind the carrel and fired at the men now charging across the room. The panicked tourists screamed and dove to the floor.

He squeezed off another round, forcing Singh's men to take cover behind the desks. Then he turned, raced after Maya. He pulled the door shut and turned the lock, but knew it wouldn't hold.

And this wasn't an exit. They were trapped in a storeroom! He glanced around and swore.

"Over here," Maya called, dragging a box to the wall. She hopped up and yanked off the cardboard covering a broken window. Grateful for her quick thinking, he rushed over and gave her a boost. She heaved the cracked window open, clambered over the ledge and leaped.

The door rattled behind him. Bullets riddled the wood. Hurrying, he hoisted himself onto the sill. The door crashed open just as he swung his legs over and jumped.

He hit the dirt, regained his balance, spotted Maya sprinting down the alley ahead. He took off behind her, but a sudden burst of gunfire razed his path. He zigzagged, lunged behind a parked rickshaw and fired back.

The shooting stopped. Silence rang in his ears. He glanced behind him, breathing heavily, and made sure that Maya was gone. Then he fired again to keep the men pinned down, and raced through the alley to catch up.

He found her waiting around the corner, her hand braced against a wall. "Back to the bookstore?" she asked, gasping.

"Yeah." They needed to find out what that inscription meant and get out of town. He ejected his spent clip, rammed another in place, then slid the gun into the holster at the small of his back. "Let's go."

She nodded, took off running, and he followed her down the busy street. Noisy trucks lumbered past. Car horns blared, punctuated by ringing rickshaw bells. He inhaled the billowing exhaust fumes, his lungs burning from the pollution as he wove through the surging crowds.

He couldn't believe the mess he'd made. Singh's men would call for backup. They'd swarm the area now. Instead of finding clues to that medallion, he'd endangered Maya more.

He was still berating himself when they reached the bookstore. He glanced down the narrow lane, making sure that the coast was clear. "Stay behind me," he ordered, then ducked inside. He paused near the door, felt a deep, unnatural silence charge the air.

He tensed, held out his arm to keep Maya back. "Wait here."

"But—"

"I said to wait."

Her eyes flashed. She opened her mouth to argue, but he ignored her and pulled out his gun. His pulse rising, focused fully on the musty bookstore, he crept forward, straining to hear. A grandfather clock ticked nearby. An electric fan whirred softly. Muted voices came from the street outside, along with the distant blaring of horns.

He wove his way through the bookcases, careful not to make any sound, then reached the counter and stopped. Books were strewn over the floor.

His belly tightened. The place had been ransacked. Singh's thugs must have followed them here.

Behind him, a floorboard creaked. He whirled around and took aim. *Maya.* He lowered the gun, and his anger flared.

"Damn it," he whispered as she stepped forward. "I could have shot you."

She winced, mouthed an apology, and his attention returned to the room. He held up his hand, signaling for her to hang back, hoping she obeyed this time.

He inched around the counter, heading toward the back. There was still no sound, no sign of the bookseller. Foreboding snaked through his gut.

He skirted another pile of books and continued down the hallway with Maya dogging his heels. The door to the back room hung open, and lamplight spilled into the hall. A dark smear glistened on the floor.

Blood.

His heart skipped. He glanced at Maya to warn her. She stared at the bloodstain, the color leached from her face. Then she stooped down and picked up a book near the trail of blood, turning the cover to show him. *Dead Languages of the Himalayas.* He nodded, and she tucked it into her pack.

"Paper?" he whispered, but she shook her head. There was no sign of the drawing they'd left.

Cursing the mess he'd mired them in, he crept toward the open door. They had no clues. Singh's men were closing in fast. And if the sketch of that inscription was gone…

He shoved away that disturbing thought, closed the final distance to the door. His weapon raised, he burst inside.

The old man lay motionless on the floor.

"Oh, God," Maya whispered from behind him.

His heart still speeding, he lowered his gun. He walked

to the body, turned it over with his foot, and his hopes shriveled.

Maya let out a strangled sound. "Is he—?"

Deven met her horrified gaze. "Yeah. He's dead."

Chapter 5

Maya gaped at the bookseller sprawled across the dusty floor, his thin gray hair matted with blood, his once-vibrant eyes vacant, his mouth frozen in a soundless scream.

She clamped her hand to her lips and closed her eyes, struggling to block out the gruesome sight. Such senseless, needless violence. And for what? A lousy book? An inscription on a good luck charm?

What on earth was going on?

She opened her eyes, averting her gaze from the lifeless man, and fought back a swell of bile. Even worse, this was her fault. It had been her idea to come here. She'd brought danger—terrible, tragic danger—to this poor, innocent man.

Sickened, she battled to compose herself, to push back the rush of remorse. She couldn't let her emotions overwhelm her—not now. She had to think, concentrate on surviving this mess. They hadn't escaped the danger yet.

Still in shock, she watched Deven prowl the room, his wide shoulders rippling with tension, the tendons standing out in his arms. He moved with power, menace, and fingered his gun with practiced ease.

A frisson of fear skidded through her, and she clutched the medallion around her neck. He looked lethal—as deadly as Sanjeet Singh. But then, he'd admitted he was a mercenary....

"Did you find the paper?" he asked, his voice low.

"Not yet." She beat back a flurry of apprehension and began to search the room. She couldn't worry about Deven now. She had to focus on why they were here.

Moving quickly, she leafed through the jumble of books, hunting through scattered papers for the sketch they'd left— but the drawing was nowhere in sight. Frustrated, she started on another pile of books. A soft thud came from the hall. She froze, shot Deven a glance. He went perfectly still.

She straightened, her eyes still on Deven, her pulse thundering in her ears. *The murderer.* What if he'd returned?

"Out back," Deven whispered, motioning toward the rear exit with his head. He turned on his heel, padded across the room toward the hall, but Maya didn't move. She wasn't about to flee and leave him to face the danger alone.

But then he sent her another hard look, jabbed his thumb toward the door, and she hesitated, suddenly unsure. Maybe he was right. Maybe she should check the alley behind the shop. What if Singh's men had surrounded the store and had them trapped?

Her pulse going crazy at that thought, she crept across the room to the door. She hoisted her pack to her shoulder, inched the door open, praying that the hinges wouldn't squeak. Then she peeked at the space behind the shop.

Empty. But she couldn't see the entire alley from here.

She glanced at Deven again. He stood dead still, his back flat against the wall, his gun ready to fire. He slashed her a glance, jerked his head for her to leave. She inhaled and stepped outside.

Every sense hyperalert, she inched away from the door. Birds chirped nearby. A clothesline flapped overhead. She scanned the graffiti-stained walls, a stack of empty crates. Farther up the alley, bags of rice were piled by a door.

Feeling vulnerable out in the open, but knowing she had to keep checking, she moved away from the shop. She padded past a large metal trash barrel, crunched over some broken glass. She stopped, swept her gaze up the deserted alley, then down to where it made a sharp bend.

Still nothing. No one was out here. She hitched out a shaky breath.

But then footsteps broke the silence, a steady slap-slap-slap coming her way.

Alarm sizzled through her. She twirled around, glanced at the bookshop door, but she didn't have time to get back. She frantically searched the alley for cover, then dove behind the trash barrel to hide.

The footsteps grew louder, closer. She curled tighter into a ball, desperate not to be seen. The steps stopped. Her lungs closed up. Her mouth went bone-dry.

Long seconds passed. The silence lengthened, stretched, an elastic band ready to snap. Unable to bear the tension, she tipped her head to the side and peeked out. A man stood by the bookshop door, holding a gun.

She ducked back behind the barrel, her pulse running amok. She had to warn Deven—but the man stood between her and the door.

And she only had seconds to act.

She scanned the area around the trash can, spotted a loose brick—too far away. And she could never throw her backpack that far. But maybe she could startle the man, get him to fire. Surely Deven would hear the shot.

She slid the pack off her shoulder and gripped the strap, waiting until the gunman stepped toward the door. Then she lunged up and hurled it at his back. He spun around and fired.

She dove to the ground behind the barrel, her heart going berserk. He hadn't hit her—but now she was trapped. He would catch her in a few short strides!

The door to the shop crashed open. A volley of gunfire deafened her ears. She peeked out, saw Deven sprinting toward her.

"Go!" he shouted.

She darted over and snatched up her backpack, ignoring the man stretched out on the stones. Then she bolted down the alley toward the street.

More shots blasted behind her. Desperate to escape the gunfire, she raced down the narrow lane. She neared the corner and Deven finally caught up.

Relief poured through her. He was safe, thank God. They veered down a narrow side street, then ran flat out toward the square, dodging bicycles and pedestrians, sprinting past beggars, scattering pigeons pecking for grain.

When they reached the bazaar they stopped, blocked by the teeming throngs. Maya hauled air to her fiery lungs, wiped her sweaty face on her sleeve. She glanced back, her nerves strung tight, but no one had caught up to them—yet.

"This way." Deven plunged into the crowd, and she hurried after, merging with the chaotic hordes. She pushed through a group of tourists, ignored a potter trying to sell her a jug. Dogs barked. Housewives haggled with farmers. A man carrying a monkey went past.

Without warning, Deven stopped. "Look by the shrine."

She craned her neck to see across the square, and her heart lurched. Several policemen stood on the shrine's brick steps, scanning the crowd. She ducked her head, leaned close to Deven, her stomach a tumult of nerves. "What now?"

"We've got to get off the streets."

But where could they hide? She had friends near here, but didn't dare involve them in this. The bookseller's murder proved that.

"Oh, hell. Keep your head down." Deven snagged her arm, towed her through the crowd.

"What is it?" she asked, smothering the urge to glance back.

"Riot police. They're heading toward us."

Riot police? Just to find them? Her lungs seized up at the thought.

They exited the square by a line of rickshaws. "Back here. Hurry," Deven urged, and she squeezed into the narrow space between the rickshaws and a building's wall. He slid in beside her, and they both hunched down.

Their shoulders touched. Deven's muscled arm pressed against hers. She tried to breathe around the tension squeezing her throat, taking comfort in his nearness, his strength.

And suddenly, she realized that even if she didn't fully trust him, even if she'd vowed never to depend on a man again, she was glad that he was along.

But then a low drumming sound filled the air. The police thundered by, their heavy boots pounding the bricks. She peeked through a gap between the rickshaws, and the sight of riot shields and flak vests caused her to blanch.

She pressed her sweating palms to her thighs and fought

down her dizzying fear. Deven was right. Singh had the police swarming the city for them. Every minute they stayed on the streets reduced their chance to survive. They had to find a place to hide, fast.

"A friend of mine lives near here," she said when the police had passed. "Indira. She'll help us."

His eyes snagged hers. "She won't talk?"

"No, she despises Singh."

His dark brows gathered. He frowned at the street, his expression reflecting his doubt. But then he nodded. "All right. But wait here while I make sure it's clear."

He crawled out from behind the rickshaws, then motioned for her to come out. Praying the police wouldn't spot them, she led the way up the street. Then she forged an erratic course through the heart of Kintalabad, taking shortcuts and detouring through alleys so no one could stay on their trail. She tried not to think about the police in close pursuit, the bookseller lying dead in his shop, the danger she might bring to her friend. But by the time they reached Indira's muddy lane, her stomach was pitching with dread.

She stopped near Indira's building, then carefully scanned the street to make sure they hadn't been tracked. A moped buzzed past. A stray dog wandered along the gutter, hunting for trash. A woman walked by, carting a basket on her head.

"How do you know this person?" Deven asked.

"She's one of the women I helped." She sent another furtive glance behind them, waited until a group of uniformed schoolboys strolled past. Then she crossed the street to her friend's apartment and rapped on the door.

Seconds later, the door cracked open, and Indira peeked out, the security chain firmly in place. A short, thin woman with cautious eyes, she looked up at Deven and paled.

Maya couldn't blame her. Deven loomed over the door like

a herald of danger—tall, heavily muscled, his dark eyes grim, his scar an angry slash. A dusting of emerging beard stubble added to his threatening look.

She stepped forward and nudged him aside. "Indira, it's me, Maya."

"Maya." Indira sounded relieved. "Come in." She unlatched the chain and ushered them inside. But when she closed the door behind them, her gaze stalled on Deven again.

"We need your help," Maya said. She sketched the situation, stressing the need for stealth, but omitted the bookseller's death. Indira's eyes grew troubled, her frown deepening as Maya spoke.

But then she turned all-business. "You must be hungry. There's food on the stove." Her gaze went to the bloody bandage on Deven's arm. "And I've got clean bandages in the bathroom."

"I'm sorry to involve you in this," Maya said, praying she'd done the right thing. "But we're desperate. We had nowhere else to go."

Indira shook her head, making her long braids sway. "Don't be ridiculous. This is nothing compared to all you've done for me."

"Can you get us different clothes?" Deven asked, holding out a wad of rupees. "Something to help us blend in?"

"Of course." She shooed the money away.

Maya hesitated, not wanting to put her out. "You're sure? You won't be late for work?"

"It will only take me a minute. There's a laundress down the street. She'll have extra clothes." She eyed Deven. "I might not find the right size, though."

"Don't worry about that. Just be careful." Suppressing a shiver, Maya rubbed her arms. "I don't think we were followed, but the police are everywhere."

"I'll hurry." Indira scurried off, and Maya locked the door behind her. Then she leaned back against it and closed her eyes. Her forehead throbbed. Her eyes felt gritty and dry. After the long night and chase through the streets, she ached to stretch out on a bed and sleep.

No chance of that, though. They had to get out of Kintalabad first. But for the moment they were safe—and alone. Her stomach fluttering at that thought, she opened her eyes and watched Deven prowl the tiny room.

"How did you meet up with her?" he asked, still looking around.

"In India." Suddenly edgy, she pushed away from the door, dropped her backpack by an ottoman, and headed into the kitchen to get the food. "Her family arranged a marriage for her when she was fourteen. But the groom turned out to be a middleman for Singh. Instead of marrying her, he sold her to a brothel."

She went to the spigot, began washing her hands. Although tragic, Indira's story played out often enough in the Himalayas. A lucrative prostitution business and desperately impoverished families contributed to the cause.

"We found her a few years later," she added as Deven joined her. "We brought her back, taught her to read. She passed her driver's test, and now she drives a taxi. She's even engaged to be married—in a love match." Which was an enormous stride forward. Most women never got past the terrible shame and degradation they'd endured.

She glanced at Deven, then flushed, realizing what she'd said. No way did she want to discuss engagements with him.

Her face still flaming, she pulled out two plates, then busied herself ladling out food. Deven washed his hands and joined her, standing far too close in the narrow space. She tried not to look his way, but from the corner of her eye she could see his hard, jeans-clad thighs, the dark hair marching up his sinewed arms, his big hands braced on his hips.

Exasperated by her obsession with him, she held out the loaded plate. "Is this enough for now?"

"Yeah." He took the plate, but didn't move, and she lifted her eyes to his. The intensity of his gaze scrambled her pulse. "So how come you never married?" he asked.

She forced a shrug. "Too busy." Hoping she sounded nonchalant, she dished out her own plate of rice. Because she wasn't about to admit how badly she'd suffered back then—the shock and disbelief, the disillusionment and hurt. That the man she'd adored—the man who'd shared her ideals, her dreams, the man who'd planned a life with her, made soul-shattering love to her—had used her, dumped her. *Lied to her.*

Her chest squeezed tight at the memory of the devastation she'd endured. Deven had done more than simply reject her. He'd forced her to confront the harsh reality that people didn't stay, at least with her. Not the parents she'd never known, not the workers at the orphanages where she'd stayed, not the man she'd loved and revered. They'd all left.

Deven had taught her to stop hoping, stop yearning, stop depending on anyone except herself. Instead, she'd dedicated herself to helping others less fortunate achieve the lives they deserved.

The love and family she'd never have.

But she didn't care about that now. She'd learned a cruel lesson, but the pain was gone. She was stronger now, content with her life. And she preferred to go it alone.

Schooling her face to reflect her indifference, she turned toward him again. His eyes were shuttered, his expression as blank as her own. And before she could stop it, her gaze roamed the craggy, male planes of his face, the sexy scruff dusting his jaw, that basely sensual mouth.

And images tore through her with the force of an elephant on a rampage—the deep rumble of his voice in the dark, his hard muscles flexing under her palms, the erotic scrape of his beard on her most intimate skin.

She swayed, plagued by the sensual memories. Her fingers turned white on her plate. So he still appealed to her. No surprises there. He'd always demolished her senses, and he'd grown even sexier with age.

But he was still the man who'd left her.

And she'd stopped dreaming years ago.

Struggling to collect herself, refusing to let him think she'd cared, she angled her chin toward the door. "Shall we eat?"

He opened his mouth, then hesitated, as if there was something more he wanted to say. Instead, he nodded, exited the kitchen, and she sagged in relief.

Determined to rein in her wayward thoughts, she settled on the ottoman across from him and dug into her food. But despite her intentions, her gaze kept gravitating to the strong, thick lines of his neck, the solid width of his shoulders stretching his T-shirt. And more memories flickered through her, unwanted images she'd repressed for years—his dark eyes simmering with hunger, that riveting way he'd watched her, the flash of his sexy grin.

She sighed, disgusted by her inability to keep her mind off him, and bolted down her food in record time. Then, while he returned to the kitchen for seconds, she retrieved her backpack and pulled out the book she'd found.

But it was in shreds. Frowning, she examined her backpack and spotted a ragged tear in the side. She looked up at Deven as he sat back down. "The book got shot."

He scowled. "You're lucky it wasn't you. That was a damned reckless thing you did back there."

She straightened her spine, annoyed by his angry tone. What right did he have to lecture her? "He was heading inside the shop. You didn't want me to warn you?"

"I didn't want you to get killed."

"Well, too bad. I don't run off and abandon people— especially when they're about to get shot."

His strong jaw worked. A muscle leaped in his cheek. And emotions flashed in his eyes—anger, frustration. Pain?

She blinked, thrown off balance by his wounded look. Why would he feel hurt? *He* was the one who'd left *her*. She was the one who'd been wronged.

She dropped her gaze to the tattered book, suddenly besieged by doubts. Why did she keep seeing that pain in his eyes? Why couldn't she shake the impression that she was missing something, that there was more to the past than she knew?

Because she was deluded, that's why. She scoffed at her wishful thinking. She knew darned well why he'd left.

And he didn't deserve her sympathy. She couldn't make excuses for him, couldn't let his potent sex appeal tempt her to revise the past.

Vowing to focus on what mattered—her medallion—she flipped through the torn-up book. She studied the shredded pages, looking for diagrams, clues, willing her mind to stay on track.

"Have you found anything?" Deven asked, still sounding annoyed.

"Not much. The pages are too torn up. I've found a few names of languages, but there's no way to know if they're the one we want."

"Nothing that matches the sketch you made?"

"No." She glanced up, jarred by a sudden worry. "You think the murderer took the paper?"

His eyes turned grim. "It's possible."

"So Singh could have it." And if the inscription was important, they'd just handed him a clue.

Shaken by that thought, knowing it was even more important to find something to go on, she paged through the rest of the book. Then she came across a cluster of fragments stuck together with blood.

She swallowed quickly, the meal she'd just eaten threatening to revolt at the sight. She tried not to think about the bookseller's glassy eyes, his splattered flesh, the stench of blood and death.

"He must have been looking at this when he was shot," she said, wrestling down another swell of nausea.

She carefully tugged apart the fragments, but halfway through the clump, she paused. "Here's something. The Abatta language. Spoken in Djanpur Province." She turned the stained scrap over. "That's all I can read."

"How about the illustration he mentioned?"

"No. There's nothing else left of the page." She double-checked the remaining pieces, then set them aside. "Judging by the bloodstains, though, this could be the language he meant."

Deven set down his empty plate and leaned forward, bracing his forearms on his knees. "You know anything about the province?"

Maya shrugged. "Just that it's remote, impoverished, rife with smugglers and outlaws. And the Forbidden Valley is there." A place where people mysteriously disappeared—and few dared go. "Why? You think someone there might know the language?"

"It's worth a try. It's the only clue we've got right now, and we need to get out of town."

She nibbled her lip. "We can ask Indira. She comes from a place near there."

A sudden knock on the door made her heart trip. Deven stood and tugged out his gun, motioning for her to stay back. Her pulse racing, she leaped to her feet and moved aside.

"It's me," Indira called, and Maya pressed her hand to her chest. Then she hurried to the door and undid the chain.

Her friend bustled in, carrying two bulging cotton bags. "I got the clothes."

"Thanks." Deven shoved his gun back into his waistband, then grabbed the bag Indira held out.

Maya took the other. "Listen, Indira. We need to get to Djanpur Province. Didn't you live near there?"

Indira's face turned ashen, her eyes wide. "You can't go there. It's too dangerous."

"We don't have much choice. We need information about an ancient language they used to speak there. Abatta. Have you heard of it?"

"No."

"Is there a village elder, someone who might know the history?" Deven pressed.

Indira hugged her arms and shook her head. "I don't know. You could ask at the monastery. Maybe the monks would know. But there's no road past Krit. The trails will be washed out this time of year. And there are insurgents, kidnappers." Indira's eyes pleaded with hers. "Believe me. You really don't want to go there."

Maya shivered, a premonition of danger sweeping through her like an icy wind. "Don't worry. We'll be fine." She hoped.

Indira gnawed her lip. She flicked her gaze to Deven, then

back to Maya again. "If you're really going to Djanpur, you need to look married. It's the only protection you'll have. Otherwise, you'll be kidnapped for sure." She crossed the room to a cabinet and pulled out a wooden box.

Realizing Indira meant to give her some jewelry, Maya held up a hand in protest. "Indira, no. I can't take that."

"I insist." She set the box on the cabinet and spread her hands. "It's not much, but it will help."

Maya's heart warmed at her generosity. She knew how precious even inexpensive trinkets were to someone who'd had nothing for years. "Thank you. I'll get them back to you. And thanks for everything—the food, the clothes. We appreciate your help so much."

Indira pressed her palms together. "I need to leave for work now, but God willing, I'll see you again." She gave Maya a quick hug, slid Deven an uneasy glance. "Don't let her out of your sight," she told him. Then she left, and the apartment door clicked shut.

Maya shivered again, trying to shake off the lingering gloom from Indira's warning, and clutched the bag of clothes to her chest. "I'll change in the bedroom."

Forcing away thoughts of danger, she grabbed her backpack, went into the sleeping alcove and pulled the curtain closed. Then she put on the long, loose pants Indira had found and the traditional tunic and shawl. She slipped the sandals on her feet, stuffed her own clothes into her backpack, using a safety pin to repair the hole. That done, she returned to the cabinet to check the box.

The mirror above the cabinet stopped her. She peered at her reflection, shrieked at her rat's nest of hair. She redid her braid, but there was nothing she could do about the shadows smudging her eyes except sleep. And she didn't have that luxury yet.

Turning her attention to the box, she sorted through the costume jewelry, choosing pieces typical for a married villager—bangles for her arms, a small gold hoop to replace the stud in her nose. She dabbed a *bindi* mark on her forehead, sprinkled red *sindoor* powder in the part of her hair like the married women did.

Then she reached back into the box and pulled out a necklace, a *pote* made of bright red, green and yellow beads— the Himalayan equivalent of a wedding ring.

Her heart faltered. Her hands trembled as she held the beads—a symbol of her hopes, her dreams, the future she'd wanted so badly with Deven.

She inhaled sharply to quell the pain. That part of her life was over. Deven meant nothing to her now. She tucked the medallion under her tunic to hide it and lifted the necklace to her throat. But a movement in the mirror caught her eye, and she paused.

Deven stood frozen behind her, his face pale, his tortured eyes on hers. And she knew what he was thinking, as clearly as if he'd shouted it out. The wedding ritual. When the groom gave the *pote* to his bride.

He should have given a *pote* to her.

She closed her eyes and swayed, unable to stop the deluge of memories—his feverish words of love, of need. How he'd cherished her, made heart-wrenching love to her, promising her forever as he made her his.

Her throat closed up. She drew in a breath, using all her strength to subdue the stinging lash of emotions. She didn't need this—not now. Not when he stood watching her. She felt too defenseless, too vulnerable, too exposed.

"I'll help with that."

Panicked, she shook her head. She couldn't handle his touch right now. "No, I…"

But he strode to her and took the necklace from her hands. She pulled her braid forward and steeled herself, unwilling to reveal how affected she was.

He draped the colored beads around her neck, then fumbled to hook the clasp. His warm fingers brushed her nape, sending shivers shimmering over her skin, and she braced herself against a torrent of pain.

His fingers stilled. She didn't move. Time seemed to grind to a halt.

"Maya." The word came out as a plea.

She forced her chin up, met his gaze in the mirror. And the agony in his eyes—the naked yearning—stripped her bare. She trembled, using all the willpower she had to hold on to her anger, her distance. *Her pride.*

She'd believed him once. She'd believed he was decent, honorable, a hero in every way.

She'd been wrong.

And she refused to delude herself again.

"Thanks," she choked out. He lowered his hands, and she turned. "Are you ready to go?"

He stared at her for an endless moment, the anguish in his eyes tearing her apart. She leaned toward him, tempted to weaken, to beg for an explanation, to believe there was some other reason he'd left.

But he turned away, added his clothes to her pack and slung it over his back. Then his eyes cut back to hers. And she saw it again—that terrible, haunting pain. "Yeah, let's go."

And despite her vow to cling to her dignity, despite her certainty that she was right, she couldn't stop the flurry of doubts. Why did she keep seeing that hurt in his eyes? Why was she so darned confused?

She knew why—because everything she'd seen of him so far supported her old view, that he was a moral, honorable man. He'd saved her from attack. He'd helped Gina escape. He was working undercover, fighting to bring down Singh.

But if he was the hero she'd once believed, then why had he callously dumped her? What secret lurked in his cynical eyes? And what was he hiding about Singh?

She crossed the room behind him, trying to forget all that and focus on the journey ahead. They had to elude the police, escape a city filled with Singh's violent thugs, cross a province fraught with danger of every type. And they were walking in blind. Singh was already a step ahead. They had no idea what they might find.

But as she pulled the shawl over her head and stepped through the door, she realized that the worst threat might not come from Singh—but the danger Deven posed to her heart.

Chapter 6

He'd failed Maya, worse than he'd ever dreamed.

Deven stood in the crowded bus depot in downtown Kintalabad, still reeling from what he'd seen. He'd expected anger from her, resentment—even indifference after all this time. But nothing had prepared him for that raw vulnerability in her eyes.

He'd intentionally hurt her when he left. Hell, he'd *wanted* to make her despise him. And all these years, he'd convinced himself that it had worked, that she'd moved on with her life, forgotten him. That she was safe and content.

But the stricken look in her eyes when she'd held that necklace had been a knife blade eviscerating his heart.

It should have been his necklace she held, the one he'd hocked the day he'd left. The one he'd promised her, along with his heart.

He fingered the old scar slashing his jaw, the proof of how thoroughly he'd failed—failed to defend his mother, failed to defeat Singh. And he'd failed to do the one thing that mattered most—protect the woman he loved.

He exhaled heavily, knowing he couldn't dwell on those troubling thoughts right now. He had to concentrate, get Maya safely out of Kintalabad—and then he could mull over the past.

"What are we going to do?" she asked from beside him.

He turned his mind to the noisy bus depot, scanning the crowded ticket counters, the weary people standing in lines. Travelers streamed past. Vendors milled around, hawking trinkets and food. Voices ebbed and rose, mingling with the hollow hand drums and reedy flutes of snake charmers entertaining a crowd.

And police guarded every door.

"We have to get on that bus." He was sure of that much. There was only one road into the mountains, and they'd stand out in a car. Their only hope was to blend in with the villagers on the local bus.

Maya nodded, but her eyes reflected her doubt. "I'd better buy the tickets. I'm less noticeable than you are."

He opened his mouth to protest, reluctant to let her go off alone. But she was right. Even with the change of clothes, his height set him apart.

"All right, but keep your head down," he warned.

She gave him a disgruntled look. "You don't have to tell me what to do. I've been hiding from Singh for years."

He scowled, not wanting to think about the risks she'd taken as the Leopard. "Don't come back here after you get the tickets. Don't even look at me. Just stay across the room. Right before the bus leaves, I'll follow you on board."

"All right."

His eyes met hers. "You have enough money?"

"Yes." She pulled the shawl closer around her face and turned.

"And, Maya…" She turned back, arched a brow. "If anything happens to me, get on that bus. Just get the hell out of town."

"But—"

"Promise me. No matter what." He'd failed her enough already. He couldn't let Singh get her now.

But her eyes narrowed, and she lifted her chin. "I told you before, Dev. I'm not the type to run off."

She spun around, plunged into the crowd, and he let out a frustrated growl. She was too stubborn, too daring.

Too appealing.

He shook off that unwelcome thought and watched her cross the room. She hunched her shoulders, assumed the weary gait of an older woman, transforming before his eyes. Then she headed straight toward a group of policemen. His gut tensed, but they barely glanced her way.

His relief mingled with reluctant respect. No wonder she'd succeeded as the Leopard. The woman knew how to blend in.

Needing to make himself less visible, he sidled through the crowd to the snake charmers and slouched against the wall to watch. A cobra coiled up from the basket, following the rhythmic movements of the charmer's flute. Feigning interest, Deven tossed a rupee into the box.

But he kept one eye on Maya as she inched through the line and bought their tickets, then huddled on a bench near the door. She looked up, and her gaze met his from across the room. He turned and walked away.

Still trying not to attract attention, he bought an apple from a vendor, wandered toward a kid performing on stilts. Joining the group of spectators, he lowered himself to his haunches and slowly hitched out his breath.

So far, so good. Maya had the tickets. No one had spotted them yet. Now they just had to get on that bus.

He bit into his apple, still wishing Maya wasn't involved in this. There were too many unanswered questions, too much he didn't know about Singh.

He knew one thing, though. Singh wouldn't let Maya go, even without the medallion, not when she'd defied him for years. He hadn't let Deven's mother escape; he'd pursued his onetime mistress for nearly two decades, refusing to let her live her own life. His high-born mother had done everything she could to evade him—changed her name, fled from town to town, performing the menial jobs of an outcast. And Singh had still caught up.

Deven rubbed his eyes to blot out the memories—his brutally tortured mother, his futile battle with Singh. Singh had slashed his face that night, then left him in the alley to die.

But Deven hadn't died. He'd lost his country, his identity, his dreams. He'd lost his illusions about his past, the future he had planned and the woman he'd loved—but he had survived.

And he'd vowed revenge.

And every day since then he'd worked to make himself stronger, more powerful. He'd honed his skills in Britain's military, toughened himself more in the Special Forces. And all the while, he'd studied how Singh thought, how he conducted business. He'd learned the man's habits and quirks. And when Interpol had needed someone to infiltrate Singh's inner circle, Deven had seized the chance.

But investigating Singh was like trying to corral snakes. Clues never panned out. He'd hit wall after dead-end wall. And when he did manage to unearth something useful, it almost seemed too easy, as if Singh had intentionally doled out the tip.

But that didn't make sense. Deven's cover had been foolproof. There was no way Singh could have recognized him, especially after all these years. And neither the head of Interpol in Romanistan nor Skinner, his Magnum boss, had known about his background. His fake identity guaranteed that.

Seething with frustration, he shook his head. Whatever Singh was up to, Deven had to stop him. He couldn't fail this time—not with thousands of lives at stake.

Especially Maya's.

An announcement blared, pulling him out of his thoughts. His bus was about to leave. He stood, tossed a coin to the kid on the stilts and carefully surveyed the room.

Police still guarded the exits. More cops roamed through the crowd. His muscles tightening with tension, he searched for Maya and spotted her looking his way. He returned his stare, willing her to follow the plan and wait for him near the bus.

Keeping his shoulders stooped, his head low, he wove toward the door through the crowd. He passed a line of beggars, vendors selling candy, bearded trekkers carting backpacks and poles.

"Hey, you," someone called from beside him. "Stop."

His pulse quickened. He kept threading his way through the throng.

"Stop. Police," the man shouted again.

He glanced back, and his heart sped up. The cop was calling to him.

He stepped over a basket of spices, dodged a woman selling beads, pretending that he didn't hear. He had to hurry, get outside the station to the lot where the buses were parked.

A whistle blew. The cop shouted at him again. He saw Maya walking toward him, and his heart abruptly lost its beat. What was she doing? She was supposed to wait by the bus.

Without warning, she lurched forward and crashed into a candy cart, causing it to overturn. Chaos broke out, a melee of people shouting, arguing, pushing. More baskets and another cart spilled.

Children swarmed the area to pick up candy. Merchants rushed to safeguard their goods. Deven glanced back and saw that the crowd had blocked the cop. The police manning the exits ran toward the fracas to help.

Deven leaped over an overturned basket and reached Maya's side. "Go," he ordered, furious that she'd disobeyed him—again. She swung around, hurried through the now-unguarded exit and he rushed after her outside.

He paused in the late-morning sunshine, spotted a bright green bus closing its doors. It rolled forward and began to drive off.

He swore, broke into a run. Maya sprinted beside him, shouting and waving her arms. But the driver refused to stop.

"Get on top," Deven yelled as the bus slowed at the end of the lot. Maya lunged for the rear bumper, grabbed hold of the metal ladder and pulled herself up. He leaped aboard a second after.

The bus accelerated, swerved around the corner. Maya gasped, and he grabbed her arm to keep her from falling off. The bus straightened, belched out a cloud of black exhaust and picked up even more speed.

"Go on up," Deven said. He glanced back, watching for signs of pursuit, but no one had followed them out. He exhaled, his heart still sprinting, then scrambled up the ladder after Maya to the roof.

Three men rode on the cargo rack. Deven followed Maya across the roof to some sacks of grain and lowered himself beside her, moving close to stake his claim.

Two of the men averted their faces. The third—a dark, wiry man smoking a cigarette—eyed Maya with a speculative gaze. Deven stared him down until he finally looked away.

But Deven wasn't about to take chances, especially with Indira's warning fresh in his mind. He shifted even closer to Maya to shelter her from prying eyes. "You all right?" he asked, his voice low.

"Yes, just out of breath." She leaned back against the sacks of rice and pulled her shawl closer around her shoulders. The wind frothed up strands of her hair.

He studied the elegant sweep of her cheekbones, the fatigue-bruised skin beneath her eyes. He wanted to hold on to his anger, to rail at her lack of sense. She'd taken a terrible risk back there, endangering herself to rescue him. But arguing with Maya was futile. She might look fragile, but she was the most independent, headstrong woman he knew.

He sighed, settled the backpack beside him, checked the gun he'd tucked into the waistband of his pants. The bus jolted through a pothole, jarring his throbbing arm, then swerved around a slow-moving truck and blasted its horn. He glanced at the bandage, saw that the wound was bleeding again. Not much he could do about that now.

"You think we're safe?" Maya asked.

"For now." Ignoring his bleeding arm, he angled back against the sacks. "You might as well rest."

She nodded and met his eyes. And for a minute time stopped, and that old camaraderie curled between them, that feeling of friendship, understanding—as if being together was right. But then her eyes flickered, and that wounded look moved through them again like a shadow passing over the earth. She crossed her arms and closed her eyes.

And emotions roiled inside him, a tumult of longing, guilt, regret. His gaze drifted over her face, her lips, the red powder of a married woman in the part of her hair—a disguise that should have been the truth.

He clamped his jaw, trying not to brood over the painful past, to force his mind to the journey ahead. They were heading into the lawless mountains, leaving all civilization behind. He had to stay alert, protect Maya at every turn.

But he also had to face the truth. He'd hurt Maya badly when he'd left. He'd let down the woman he'd loved.

And she deserved to know the truth. He had to explain why he'd left her that night, the events that had changed both their lives. But not yet, not here.

And not all of it. Not the part that would disgust her, the secret he would take to his grave.

Because in truth, he'd hadn't left only to keep her safe from Singh—but to protect her from himself.

A deep sense of unease woke Maya late that afternoon.

She opened her eyes, blinking at the gunmetal clouds seething above her, the steep, forested hills that flanked the winding road. The fragrance of pines filled the cool, mountain air. The bus vibrated roughly beneath her, its engine screaming as it slowed for a curve, and she clutched the cargo rack to keep from sliding away.

And memories rushed back—the bookseller's glassy eyes, the page fragments splattered with blood, that ominous sense of danger that had plagued her dreams.

She pressed her hand to her chest, feeling for the medallion beneath her tunic, then sagged back in relief. She hadn't lost it, thank God. But that sinister feeling of dread, that whisper of imminent evil still plucked at her nerves.

She sat up straighter and glanced at Deven beside her. His jaw was covered with a day's growth of whiskers, his forehead furrowed as he looked out at the hills. His loose cotton shirt flapped in the breeze, emphasizing the muscular breadth of his back.

He turned his head, as if sensing her watching, and the tension in his eyes worried her more. "What's wrong?"

"The bus is stopping."

"Why? Is there a village?"

"I don't think so."

The bus lurched again, the engine whining in protest as the driver downshifted gears. Turning, Maya scanned the densely wooded hills bordering the road ahead. But there were no huts, no other buildings or trails. No reason they should stop. Except—

"There's a roadblock," Deven confirmed.

Her alarm growing, she leaned out and spotted a wooden barrier surrounded by police vans several curves ahead. Had Singh set this up? Her pulse ran amok at the thought.

"Come on," Deven said. "We need to get off before it stops."

Her gaze darted to the men perched on the cargo rack, and she lowered her voice. "What about them? What if they tell the cops?"

"We don't have a choice. If we don't get off, they'll catch us for sure." He picked up the backpack and rose.

Maya staggered to her feet behind him, trying to balance on the swaying bus. Then she stumbled across the roof to the ladder, ignoring the curious looks of the men.

Deven headed down first. Halfway down, he stopped and held out his hand. "Here. Hold on to me."

"I'm fine. Go on." She waved him off, scooted to the edge of the ladder, waiting while he climbed down the rungs. Then she turned, adjusted her grip on the metal railing, and began to descend.

A hand seized her wrist.

She snapped up her head and stopped. A man leered over the side—the same one who'd stared at her earlier on. "Let go," she demanded. "I'm getting off."

"Why the rush?" He bared his tobacco-stained teeth. "Maybe you don't want the cops to see you? Maybe you need my protection to keep them away?"

She struggled to jerk her hand loose. He clasped her wrist tighter, annoying her even more. She wasn't about to let this creep detain her. She pulled back and twisted hard.

But the wiry man was stronger than he appeared. His nails bit into her skin. He continued pulling, trying to haul her back up. Outraged, she hooked her foot in the ladder's rung to stay in place. "I said to let go," she gritted out, but he just laughed.

She glanced down, saw Deven waiting below her, poised to leap off the slowing bus. Growing desperate, she yanked her arm back, but still couldn't get him to budge.

"Come on," Deven called up, sounding impatient.

"I can't. This guy—"

"Oh, hell." Deven started back up the ladder, sudden fury etched on his face.

But she'd already had enough. Before the man could guess her intention, she lunged up and bit down hard on his hand. He screamed, let go.

She flew down the metal ladder, burning her palms on the rails, crashing into Deven on the bottom rung. She clung to the railing, fighting to keep her balance, afraid she was going to fall off. Deven grabbed her arm to steady her, and she turned to face the road.

The bus slowed for another bend. Her pulse raced even more. "You ready?" Deven asked.

"Yes." Knowing every second counted, she inched across the bumper, inhaled deeply for courage, then leaped toward the side of the road. She hit the grass, her knees slamming into the ground, and cried out at the sharp stab of pain.

But Deven rushed over a heartbeat later. "Run!" He hauled her up, pulling her into motion. She stumbled, nearly fell, but managed to regain her feet.

A shout came from behind them. *The police.* Her heart galloping, she barreled after Deven up the hill.

"This way." He dropped her arm, sprinted into the woods, and she followed, her breath rasping out of control. A shot barked out, and she accelerated even more.

Fueled by adrenaline, she trampled ferns, plowed past dense, prickly nettles, knowing she couldn't risk slowing down. But the hill was slippery, wet from the recent rains. She tripped on a log and fell.

She shoved aside the twigs poking her face and hauled herself upright. Then she charged after Deven, dodging branches and trees.

But she was too tired, the hill too steep, and her sandals made it hard to run. She skidded again, nearly losing her balance. Branches whipped and stung her face.

She'd never make it. They were going to get captured—and it was her fault. That man never would have delayed her if she hadn't refused Deven's help.

Her legs spasmed and trembled. She wheezed in big gasps of air. A roar rose above the blood pressure pounding her skull, along with the shouts of approaching men.

Then suddenly, Deven stopped. She careened forward,

propelled by her momentum, and crashed into his out‐
stretched arm.

"What…?" She glanced at where he was looking and
spotted the source of the roar. A river raced through the trees
ahead—a vast, angry river—swift, wide, treacherous, churning
with deadly rapids, swollen from the recent monsoons.

There was no way they could cross it. It was too big, moving
too fast. They'd die if they even tried.

The voices grew louder behind them. Another gunshot
whizzed by. She spun back to Deven and saw the terrible truth
in his eyes.

They were trapped.

Chapter 7

Maya gaped at the torrent thundering past in a savage rampage—colliding with boulders, ripping trees loose and tossing them around like twigs. Trying to cross that river would be suicidal—but what else could they do? The police were gaining on them, crashing through the woods, just yards away. They had minutes at most to escape.

She swallowed hard, unable to steady her voice. "We have to get across."

"But not here. Come on." Deven broke into a run, and she followed, still scanning the swollen shores. But the river roared and seethed—boiling with rapids, clawing chunks of earth off the banks. And the opposite shore was nearly a thousand feet away—as unreachable right now as the moon.

They could never swim across; the current would sweep them away. And the chances of finding a bridge in the wilderness were nil. But there had to be a solution. They couldn't let the police catch them now!

Then suddenly, she spotted some logs jammed against the rocks. She stopped, squinting, caught by their uniform shape. "Deven, look. I think there's a raft."

Her hopes surging, she skidded down the bank to the river, her certainty growing with every step. It was a raft, all right—about ten feet square, lashed together with rusted wire. But several logs dangled at an awkward angle, on the verge of breaking off.

"What do you think?" she asked Deven when he caught up.

"I'll be surprised if it floats." He climbed over the rocks, shoved the raft back into the river and stepped on board. The makeshift raft dipped, riding perilously low in the water, but at least it didn't sink. "The damned thing's going to break apart," he muttered, grabbing a branch to use as a pole.

He was right, but what choice did they have? "We have to risk it. There's no other way across."

A shot rang out. She flinched, pivoted back, spotted three policemen racing down the hill. Her pulse rocketing, she scooped up a waterlogged branch, grabbed Deven's outstretched hand and climbed aboard.

The raft tilted, sinking lower under her added weight, sending icy water lapping over her feet. She shivered, positioned her branch against the rocks next to Deven, and pushed. The raft tipped even more.

She dropped to her knees for balance and continued to shove with her pole. Deven grunted beside her, his arm muscles bulging. The raft slid back and broke free.

They drifted away from the bank, made a languid turn, and began to pick up speed. Maya glanced back just as a cop raised his gun and fired. She ducked, her heart thrashing in her throat. He'd missed—but they still weren't out of range.

But Deven dropped to one knee and whipped out his own

gun. The police scattered, diving for cover—buying them time. The raft twirled again, rocking dangerously as the current seized it. They moved faster, rounded a bend in the river and left the police behind.

Her ears still ringing from the gunshots, Maya pressed her hand to her erratic heart. "That was close."

Deven didn't answer. She shot her gaze to his face. He scowled at the seething maelstrom, his face muscles rigid with tension, harsh grooves bracketing his mouth.

And she knew what he wasn't saying. The danger had just begun.

The current seized the flimsy raft, then moved them deeper into the river at a dizzying speed. The logs rippled and bobbed, sloshing icy water over her knees.

"We've got to get to the other side," he shouted over the river's din. He stuck his pole in the water, shook his head. "Too deep."

Shivering, she clutched her now-useless pole. They had no way to steer, no way to control the raft. And if that wire didn't hold, and the raft broke apart or sank…the current would either pull them under or dash them against the rocks.

The water thundered past. Trees on the bank flew by. She stared at the deadly current, knowing she had to keep them afloat. The frigid spray soaked her clothes.

Suddenly, a boulder appeared ahead. "Watch out!" she cried.

Deven whipped around and jabbed at the boulder with his pole, but they still crashed into the side. The raft shuddered, dipped precariously, threatening to break apart. More water washed over the logs.

But miraculously, they didn't sink. They scraped by another rock, continued careening along. Maya clung to the wet, icy wood, cringing as the carcass of a goat floated by, feeling helpless and out of control.

A feeling she'd always despised—except in Deven's arms.

The stray thought zinged out of nowhere, catching her off guard. She glanced at Deven kneeling beside her, his eyes burning with concentration, his jaw hewn from stone. His hair was soaked, slicked back from his rugged face, his wet clothes plastered to his muscular frame. He radiated power, single-minded intensity.

And beyond the fear gripping her nerves, beyond her anger over the past, she had to acknowledge the truth. Deven had always made her feel safe. He'd made her feel treasured, desired, *wanted*—a lure an abandoned child couldn't resist.

She jerked her gaze to the turbulent water. She didn't want to remember the rapture. She didn't even want to like him again—because no matter how strong or attractive he was, that desire had only been fleeting, his promises had only been lies.

And therein lay the danger. There was something different about Deven. Something compelling. He had the power to make her lower her defenses, to evoke long-buried feelings and needs—the yearning for a family, love. *Him*.

"Look out!" he shouted.

Startled, she glanced up, saw a huge tree barreling toward the raft. Her mind went blank with fear.

"Push off!" Deven leaped to his feet and jabbed at the tree with his pole, trying to keep it from smashing the raft. Her pulse frantic, she added her own branch, struggling to turn it away. The raft bobbed, tipped up. She shoved with all her might. Sweat beaded her face despite the cold.

The tree changed course, and the raft spun free. She

slumped back on her heels, rattled by the narrow miss. If that tree had hit them, they could have died.

But then a deep noise pierced her awareness. She tensed, listening hard, and realized the tenor of the river had changed. It sounded angrier, even more threatening. "What's that noise?"

Deven jerked around and swore. "It's a waterfall."

A waterfall? She gaped at the swirling river—and realized he was right. The current was changing, sucking everything toward the center, moving even faster as it raced downstream.

"We have to jump off," he yelled over the river's noise.

Jump off? She stared at him in shock. "It's too far. We need to get closer to shore."

"There's no time. Swim at an angle toward those rocks." He pointed to the opposite shore. "And don't put your feet down. They could get trapped if there's any debris. Now go!"

She quailed at the dark, frothing water. Thunderous booms punctuated the roar. No way did she want to go in there. But Deven was right. There wasn't time.

She slipped off her sandals, clutched them in her hand so she wouldn't lose them, then plunged into the torrent and shrieked. The current instantly swept her downstream— heading straight for the falls.

Her nerves erupted with panic. She struck out toward the shore, swimming with a vengeance, angling toward the jumble of rocks. But the raging river tore at her hair and clothes with relentless force, threatening to suck her back in.

She gulped in mouthfuls of water, battling to stay afloat. Keeping her head up, her feet raised, she thrashed toward the opposite shore.

Her arms ached. The freezing water numbed her skin. But she forced herself to continue, arm over arm, yard after yard, until she'd nearly reached the shore. She made a final lunge, closed the distance to the rocks, then collapsed against them in relief.

But where was Deven? She glanced around, her teeth chattering, but he was nowhere in sight. She dragged herself onto a rock with effort, her muscles twitching with exhaustion, so cold she could hardly breathe.

And then she saw him—bobbing ten yards away near a clump of rocks. His head went down, pushed by the current. Sputtering, he came back up. He was trapped!

She didn't hesitate. Tossing her sandals onto the bank, she leaped back into the river and swam frantically toward him, battling the current trying to pull her downstream. "Deven!"

He looked up, caught her eye. "Stay back!" he shouted. "You'll go over the falls."

She ignored him, kept swimming toward him, terror fueling her strokes. Suddenly, the current grabbed her, sucking her under. She clawed back up and gasped for air, her arms so tired she could hardly float. But she had to reach Deven. He would drown if she didn't help.

She made another violent thrust and reached his side, then crashed against the rocks. She ignored the pain stinging her shoulder, bracing herself to stay up. "Where are you caught?"

"Here." He shoved at a rock but it didn't budge. She added her strength, heaving with all her might. It teetered, fell back. They pushed and it tipped again. Maya grunted, strained. The rock toppled, and Deven broke free.

But the current seized her, began to drag her away. She cried out, reached blindly for Deven, and he managed to grab her hand. Then, still holding on to her, he towed her toward the shore.

The water swirled and crashed against them. Maya tried to swim, but her limbs had grown too cold to move. Endless minutes passed as the river churned around them, and her helpless feeling grew.

But amazingly, they reached the bank. Deven stood in the shallow water and pulled her to her feet. She staggered behind him out of the river and collapsed in a clump of weeds.

Her stomach heaved. She pressed her face to the grass, trembling uncontrollably, so frozen she couldn't think. Deven crawled closer, threw his arm around her back and cradled her in his arms.

For an eternity, they just lay there. Overcome with exhaustion, Maya wheezed in air and shivered wildly, her emotions spinning out of control.

"You all right?" he rasped into her ear.

"Just…c-cold," she gritted out, her teeth clacking hard.

"You're lucky to be alive." Sudden anger vibrated his voice. "Can't you ever follow orders? Don't you realize how dangerous that was?"

"But you…you would have…" She shook her head, unable to finish the thought.

He held her tighter, and she closed her eyes, taking comfort in his warmth, his strength, the security of his arms. But even the most powerful man could die.

And if she'd lost him… She shuddered, not wanting to examine the panic that thought provoked.

And suddenly, the enormity of their predicament hit her. The police were hunting them like animals. Singh was trying to kill them. He would never give up—no matter how many people lost their lives. And now, in that river, they'd nearly died.

Her eyes burned. Her chest ached. She tried to beat back

the weakness, hating this urge to cry. But God, that had been so close…

Deven swore, pulled her tighter against him and rested his cheek against hers. And for long moments she just huddled in his arms, savoring the power of his tough, male body, the reassuring beat of his heart.

She knew this embrace meant nothing. He was holding her out of basic human kindness, giving comfort after a disaster, nothing more.

But then why did he feel so safe, so virile…so arousing?

She blinked, tried not to go there. But his big hand crept to her neck, sending awareness skipping through her nerves. Her breath turned uneven. Her blood made a ragged charge. He pulled back slightly, and she turned her head and met his eyes.

His hot, hungry eyes.

Her breath backed up. She couldn't move. She was riveted by the drops of water forging trails down his whiskered cheeks, the undisguised need in his eyes.

His gaze dropped to her lips. Her heart nearly burst from her chest. And suddenly, she wanted desperately to kiss him, to feel his mesmerizing mouth on hers. To forget the danger, forget the past, just give in to the moment and live.

He lowered his head and moved his mouth over hers, and every cell in her body went berserk. His kiss was warm, gentle, familiar and yet different somehow—like a forgotten dream, a wispy memory that had lingered at the fringes of her mind.

And now came blazing back to life.

She ran her hands up his steel-band arms, inhaled the scent of his wet, male skin. The sensual scrape of his beard, the hard muscles tensing under her palms sent heat pooling deep in her loins.

His kiss grew longer, more insistent. His tongue swept

her lips, and she opened to him, drawing him in. He pressed against her, flattening her against the grass, and her head began to spin.

She wanted him closer, harder, everywhere. She wanted his hands on her naked skin, his mouth on her aching breasts. She shuddered as the hunger consumed her, as long-dormant needs exploded to life.

But he broke the kiss and rested his forehead against hers. And she struggled to calm her erratic heart, to battle the delirium blanking her mind, the urge to toss caution away.

Then he loosened his arms and sat back. "Maya…" His reluctance was clear in his voice.

She closed her eyes against a flash of pain. Of course he regretted that kiss. Holding her had been instinctive, a reaction to the danger they'd shared. And she'd gone off the deep end, taking it out of control.

"We need to go," he said. "It'll be dark soon."

"You're right." They were cold, soaked, exhausted. The backpack—with their spare clothes—was gone. They had no food, no water to drink. Deven's arm was bleeding, her own body pummeled and scraped. And at this elevation, the night would turn frigid fast. They had to find shelter before they froze.

He stood, pulled her to her feet, and their gazes collided again. And she couldn't stop the desire surging through her, that traitorous hunger weakening her knees.

But he dropped her hand and turned away. Still shivering, she retrieved her sandals from where she'd left them and trudged after him up the slope.

So nothing had changed. This man still demolished her senses, even after all these years. Everything about him appealed to her—his wicked eyes, his granite frame, that blatantly sexual kiss… The way he protected her, watched out for her… The camaraderie they shared.

But none of that mattered. He didn't want her. He never had. No matter how much he tempted her, she couldn't weave fantasies about him again.

And she definitely couldn't give in to the urge to kiss him again. That had been foolish, dangerous. It had opened the floodgates, awakened carefully stifled needs, making her yearn for things she could never have.

And that was a risk she couldn't take. She'd barely survived his rejection once. The next time would demolish her heart.

But no matter how hard she tried to forget it, she couldn't drive that kiss from her mind. Even two hours of brutal climbing—hacking through dense undergrowth, clambering up slopes so steep she grew light-headed if she chanced to glance down—did nothing to quiet her thoughts. She ping-ponged from desperately wanting to kiss him again, to knowing she shouldn't touch him, to hungering to relive those thrills. By the time they reached the cave he'd found, she felt like a banyan seed buffeted by a fickle wind.

He stopped, and she staggered to a halt behind him. The cave sat halfway up the side of the mountain, a black maw nearly obscured by trees. In front stretched a small stone ledge.

He held out his arm to keep her back. "Wait here while I check it out."

She nodded, too exhausted to argue, and shivered in the gathering dusk. The fire ring on the ledge outside the cave was darkened with scorch marks, indicating someone had recently stayed here. Recalling Indira's warning about outlaws, she scanned the surrounding woods.

But a moment later, Deven strode back out. "It's empty. And we're in luck. They left supplies."

"Do you think it's safe to stay here? What if the people come back?"

"It's riskier not to. We need to warm up." His gaze cut to hers. And memories of that kiss blazed back in shocking detail—the sexy rasp of his whiskers, the exciting sweep of his tongue.

Her face flamed, and she tore her gaze away. Talk about warming up… But she couldn't dwell on that kiss just now. They had far more serious troubles to deal with—hunger, dehydration, exhaustion. Even Deven had started to slow.

Resolved to do her part, she crossed the stone ledge and entered the cave, then paused for her eyes to adjust to the gloom. She sucked in the dank, cool air, rubbed the goose bumps rising on her arms.

"I'll get a fire going," Deven said from behind her. "Why don't you change out of those wet clothes, then look for food?"

"Won't the fire attract attention?"

He glanced around at the trees. "We're pretty well hidden. We'll be fine for a while."

"All right." Blowing on her stiff hands to warm them, she took a quick tour of the cave. It was about twenty feet deep, dank and cold, with moisture beading the walls. But in the back she found a treasure trove of supplies—blankets, a pile of men's clothes.

She glanced at the ledge, made sure Deven had his back to her as he gathered wood. Then, shivering violently, she stripped off her soaked clothes, tugged on a long shirt and woolen socks, and wrapped a blanket over her back. She took her wet clothes outside, wrung them out and spread them over the rocks.

Her teeth still chattering, she watched Deven build the fire. The sparks smoldered on the damp kindling, then finally flickered to life. He added more slivers of wood, his face bronzed by the growing glow. And his male beauty washed through her again—that thick black hair, his virile face, those arresting, carnal eyes.

He glanced up, and his gaze clashed with hers, knocking her pulse off course. Appalled at herself, she stalked back into the cave. She had to focus on keeping them alive, not ogle her ex-fiancé.

She was in luck. Hidden behind a bedroll, she found a plastic container with tea, strips of jerky made from water buffalo meat and packets of dried lentil soup. She grabbed a tin pot, a bottle of drinking water and cups, then carted the treasure outside.

Deven rose and helped her with the supplies. She knelt beside him, careful to avoid meeting his eyes. "There are more clothes and blankets in the back." She unscrewed the cap on the water bottle and sniffed. "I'll boil water for soup while you change."

"Sounds good." He strode into the cave, and she took advantage of his absence to compose herself. By the time he returned—his feet and torso bare, a blanket riding low on his hips, she had the soup made and her thoughts firmly under control.

She wished. She perched on the ledge beside him, sipping her steaming soup, basking in the warmth of the flames. But her eyes kept returning to his gilded shoulders and arms, the ribbon of black hair arrowing down his abs, the sensual gleam of his skin.

She pulled the blanket closer around her and stifled a sigh. And the memory of that sizzling kiss…

"Any idea where we are?" she asked to distract herself.

He shrugged, drawing her gaze to his powerful shoulders again. "It depends on how far we traveled on that raft. If we're not in Djanpur Province, we must be close." He pointed to a snowy peak barely visible in the dusk. "That's Mount Sangkat. The monastery's at its base. I'm guessing we'll reach it in a day or two, assuming we find a trail."

She munched another piece of jerky, mesmerized by his hands as he reached for his gun. He took the weapon apart, dried the pieces with the edge of his blanket, then reassembled it with stunning speed.

A mercenary, indeed.

"There's probably a village nearby," he added after a moment. "These supplies had to come from somewhere. We'll look for a trail at first light."

She nodded, comforted by his logic. "You think the police will keep looking for us?"

He lifted his broad shoulders again. "They won't know how far we went. That buys us some time. Even if they send out dogs, the water will mask our scent."

She shuddered, not wanting to think of police dogs scouring the hills for them, or their harrowing ride in that raft. "I can't imagine that my medallion is that important."

He sighted down his pistol, then placed it by the wad of rupees he'd set out to dry. "Mind if I look at it?"

She hesitated, reluctant to take it off. But no matter what Deven had done in the past, no matter how many secrets he kept, she knew she could trust him with this. She tugged it off, handed it to him.

He cradled the charm in his hand, examined it by the flickering light. The dancing flames made the silver gleam, and burnished his inky hair. Her gaze roamed the hollows of his cheeks, the corded sinews of his powerful neck, the way the firelight varnished his skin. Realizing she was ogling him again, she sighed.

He flipped the medallion over, studied the inscription on the back. "I'm surprised you still have this. What made you keep it after all this time?"

She pulled her gaze to the twisting flames. "Lots of reasons, I guess. For one thing, I've always had it. It would seem strange not to wear it after all these years. And it's a good luck charm. I hate to think I'm superstitious, but…" She shrugged. "You never know, right?"

"Right." He leaned over and handed it back. Their fingers touched, and a sensual jolt heated her skin. Not wanting him to see her reaction, she kept her gaze on the medallion, tracing the familiar figure of Parvati with her thumb. Bracelets snaked up the goddess's arms. A sacred thread hung between her bare breasts. Her eyes were knowing, wise, comforting.

"And the other reason?" he asked.

"What?" She looked up.

"Why else have you kept the medallion? You said there were several reasons."

She frowned, debating whether to tell him. He'd probably laugh if he knew. But maybe it was the fatigue—or maybe it was the harrowing, near-death journey down that river—but she didn't feel up to evading the truth.

"Someone gave this to me," she said. "I don't know who it was, maybe just a stranger who felt sorry for an orphaned child. But when I was little, I pretended that it came from my family, that it was a link to them, a connection to the people I never knew." To someone who might have loved her—a sign that despite the misery of her life, despite the terrible human predators she'd fended off in the streets, there was someone good out there, someone who cared.

"And after a while… I don't know. I guess it became a

symbol of the roots I never had. The family I wanted to have."
The future she'd yearned for with him—marriage, children,
a home.

His gaze held hers. "But you never married."

"No, I never married." Feeling exposed suddenly and
sensing she'd revealed too much, she slipped the chain over
her head and stood.

But Deven got to his feet and blocked her way. "Why not?
Why didn't you marry? And don't give me that bull about not
having time."

His demanding tone sparked her temper. "Why do you
care? You left me, remember? It's none of your business what
I did."

"Just answer the question, Maya."

And suddenly, she'd had enough. She was too tired, too
goaded to hide the truth. "You know why. Because I'm not
the kind of woman men want."

"What?"

"You heard me." Her pride gone, her emotions stripped
bare, she moved around him and headed toward the cave.

"Maya, wait." His ragged voice slowed her steps. She
paused and closed her eyes, struggling to quell the fierce ache
mauling her chest, to pick up her tattered pride. She crossed
her arms, forced herself to turn around.

His face was backlit by firelight, his hands clenched into
fists. "How can you say that?" His voice was anguished, raw.
"Any man would want you."

"You didn't." And he was the only man she'd ever loved.
The one man she couldn't have.

She turned and entered the cave in defeat.

Chapter 8

The lonely hoot of an owl woke Maya from a restless sleep sometime near dawn. The cold mountain air seeped through her bones. Her shoulder ached from hours spent lying on the hard stone ledge. Several feet away, the low fire flickered in the still-black night, enveloping her in a circle of golden light.

She watched the banked fire shimmer and glow, then lifted her gaze to Deven sitting across from her, staring into the flames. Wearing his now-dry clothes, he sat with one leg drawn up, his forearm braced on his knee. The cloth bandage he'd tied around his wounded biceps peeked out from beneath his short sleeve.

She never should have revealed the truth to him. She'd exposed too much, confessed to her deepest shame. And for what? It hadn't changed the past, hadn't altered his feelings for her. She'd only humiliated herself and resurrected the pain.

He picked up a piece of wood and fed it into the fire.

Flames crackled and licked at the branch, sending smoke curling into the air. She gazed at his high, flat cheekbones, his blue-black hair, the way the firelight lapped at his skin.

He was a gorgeous man, all hard muscles and rugged strength. She wondered again what secrets he kept, the cause of the pain she'd glimpsed in his eyes. What it was about him that drew her, tempting her to ignore how he'd left her in the past.

As if sensing her scrutiny, he looked up. Their gazes caught across the fire. And she saw emotions flit through his eyes— weariness, guilt, regret.

"Maya…" he began.

"Didn't you sleep?" No way did she want to discuss the past again. Her pride had been ravaged enough.

"Some." He speared his hand through his uncombed hair. "Listen. About that night—"

"Forget it. It doesn't matter."

"The hell it doesn't."

She sat up, pulled the blanket closer around her shoulders and forced herself to meet his eyes. "Deven, it happened years ago. We were kids. There's no need to dredge all that up."

"I still want to explain."

She returned her gaze to the glowing embers, the shimmering bursts of red and orange. So he wanted to unburden his conscience. Everything inside her rebelled at the thought. But maybe it would do some good. They were stuck in this ordeal together, at least for a few more days. Maybe they should clear the air—even if it did flay her pride.

She lifted one hand, let it drop. "Fine. Go ahead and tell me why you left."

He didn't answer right away. The owl hooted again in the distance. The undergrowth rustled nearby. A breeze whispered past, stirring up sparks from the fire, making the pine branches creak overhead.

"You remember that night?" he finally asked, his voice low.

As if she could ever forget.

Suddenly needing distance, she got up, gathered the blanket around her and walked away from the fire. At the end of the narrow ledge, she stopped and stared into the night.

He'd come to her under the cover of darkness, on a moonless night like this one, his eyes simmering with hunger, the planes of his face drawn tight. She'd been waiting for him, scared that he wouldn't come, even more terrified that he would.

She closed her eyes, swallowed hard at the images branded in her brain—his golden skin glistening in the candlelight, the exciting urgency of his touch. He'd been the perfect lover— reverent, intense, insatiable—worshipping her with his hands, his body, his lips. And she'd opened to him, surrendered herself completely. She hadn't held anything back.

Endlessly patient, ruthlessly sensual, he'd brought her to peak after shattering peak. And that glorious instant when his restraint had burst, and he'd lost all control…

She let out a heavy sigh. It had been the most thrilling night of her life.

The next day had been the worst.

She folded her arms, forcing herself to remember. She'd been surprised at first when he hadn't shown up at her house. As the day wore on she'd grown worried, afraid he'd been injured or ill. Finally she'd rushed to his apartment, sick with anxiety—and found it vacant, completely cleared out.

She'd been stunned, shocked, unable to believe that he'd vanished, that he'd left with no message, no explanation, just slunk off during the night.

And she'd waited for him for weeks, hoping beyond reason

that he would return, unwilling to admit that this admirable man had lied. But eventually, she'd had to accept the facts. Reality had set in, demolishing any lingering hopes she'd had. And she'd picked up the pieces of her shattered life—a life that no longer included him.

Deven came up behind her. Her chest heavy with the painful memories, she kept her gaze on the formless night.

"Do you remember?" he asked again, his voice rough.

"Yes, I remember."

"I meant what I said that night. I wanted to marry you. I didn't want to go. I *had* to. It was the only way I could keep you safe."

"Safe?" Surprised, she looked up. "From what?"

"Singh."

Singh. The bleakness in Deven's voice made her blood chill. She searched his face, saw the truth in his tortured eyes. And suddenly, everything she'd believed about the way he'd left her was thrown in doubt. She flashed back to the night she'd escaped Singh's palace, when Deven had warned her about probing the past. He'd sounded just as lonely, just as despairing then….

"What did Singh do?"

"He was at my apartment when I got home that night. He'd murdered my mother."

Shock rippled through her. Singh had murdered his mother—and Deven had seen it? She pressed her fingers to her lips. "Oh, Deven. I'm so sorry." She couldn't even imagine how horrific that must have been. "But…why?"

He exhaled. "She was his mistress when she was young—but not by choice. Her family had arranged their marriage, not knowing he had a wife. By the time she figured out he was a bigamist, it was too late."

Maya could believe it. She'd seen men do worse.

"She tried to leave him, but he wouldn't let her go. So she escaped, went on the run." His gaze met hers. "That's how I grew up, always on the run with her, frequently changing my name. She feared for her life, knew he'd kill her if he ever caught up. And she was right. He didn't give up, even after all that time. That night...I got home too late. I couldn't save her."

The horror of it engulfed her. Of course he would blame himself. While he'd been making love to her, his mother had lost her life.

"What did you do?" she whispered.

"I tried to fight him, but he was too strong." His hand went to the long scar crossing his jaw. "I managed to escape, but I knew he'd come after me—and you, to get to me. I took her wedding necklace, her *pote*. Not Singh's—she'd pawned that one long ago—but the one that had been handed down through her father's family." His eyes turned bleak. "The one I'd intended to give to you. I sold it."

The pain in his voice brought a terrible ache to her throat. So he really had cared. He hadn't lied.

His eyes turned distant, lost in the past. "I used the money to buy a new identity. I got a British passport, flew out the same day. When I got to England, I joined the army and went to Iraq. Eventually I got recruited into the Special Forces, the Special Reconnaissance Regiment. And from there to Magnum, the company I work for now."

He made it sound simple, but she could only imagine how hard, how lonely that must have been. "But why would Singh have followed you? You weren't to blame for what your mother did?"

"I had something he wanted. It's complicated...dangerous. I can't tell you more than that. But after the way he'd pursued my mother, I knew he wouldn't give up. He'd go after anyone

I knew to get me. I wanted to tell you, to say goodbye, but I couldn't risk it. If anything had happened to you… Believe me, Maya, if there had been any other way…"

She pulled her gaze to the darkness beyond the ledge, her mind spinning with his revelation, still grappling to absorb it all. But she believed him. Except for the night that he'd left her, she'd known him to be an honorable man. Even now he'd protected her, saving her at every turn. And she couldn't doubt that pain in his voice.

He moved closer, his eyes filled with remorse. "It damned near killed me to leave you," he admitted. "And I thought about you all the time. But I couldn't tell you the truth. And I'd hoped… I'd hoped you'd move on, that you'd find someone else, someone who deserved you. Someone better than me."

Her heart wobbled hard. She read the truth of his words in his eyes. This strong, courageous man had exiled himself to keep her safe. And he didn't believe he deserved her now.

"I'm not asking for forgiveness," he continued, his voice somber. "I'd do the same again. And you're right to despise me. I don't expect that to change. But for God's sake, Maya, don't *ever* think I didn't want you."

Her eyes misted with tears. A huge lump lodged in her throat. She blinked quickly, battling back the swarm of emotions, trying not to overreact. This didn't erase the past. It didn't even change the future. There was still too much he hadn't explained—such as what he'd taken from Singh. But it did alter her perspective, forcing her to rethink the conclusions she'd formed.

"Thank you for telling me," she whispered. She raised her trembling hand, traced the silvery scar marring his face. "And I don't despise you."

His eyes glittered, and he caught her wrist. "You should.

I'm not a good man, Maya. There are things about me you still don't know."

"I know enough."

Their eyes stayed locked. Emotions arced between them— understanding, sorrow for all they'd lost. And something deeper, something far more elemental.

He turned his head, his eyes still riveting hers, and brushed her wrist with his lips. Her pulse ran amok. Her belly fluttered with nerves.

He dropped her wrist and shifted closer, drawing her into his arms. His big, rough hands cupped her face. His long legs bracketed hers. Electrified by his nearness, she forgot to breathe.

And then he lowered his head and kissed her—softly, tenderly, as if expressing his regrets.

Buffeted by sensations, she melted against him. She savored the sensual heat of his mouth, inhaled the intriguing scent of his skin. He angled her chin, parted her lips with his tongue, igniting a tempest of need in her blood.

This was the man she'd lost, the man she'd loved. The man who was better than he'd admit.

He ended the kiss, but didn't move. His thumb stroked her throat. His uneven breath battled with hers.

And raw need blazed in his eyes.

"Maya, walk away," he rasped.

She trembled, knowing she should do it. The past was gone. They had no future together. This was a line they shouldn't cross.

But this was a night of truth, a night without pretense. She'd bared her soul, revealed her vulnerability and pain. And Deven had allowed her a glimpse of the darkness he had inside.

He lowered his hands to her hips and tugged her close. And

even through the blanket, she could feel his arousal prodding the apex of her thighs.

No lies. No deceptions. Just brutal honesty.

He wanted her, needed her.

She didn't have it in her to refuse.

"Make love to me, Deven."

His fingers flexed on her hips. The muscles of his whiskered throat worked. "You're sure?"

"Yes." She was sure. This man had always felt right.

He closed his eyes, shuddered hard, as if battling for self-control. And then, like a volcano erupting, he jerked her against him, taking her lips in a hard, plundering kiss that wiped out every thought.

His steel-hard body pressed against hers. His powerful shoulders rippled and bunched. He ravaged her mouth with his tongue, sparking a riot of delirious sensations, wrenching a moan from her throat.

And she kissed him back with reckless abandon. She stroked his face, his shoulders, his back. She savored his warmth and strength, wanting him everywhere, giving vent to the hunger she had smothered for years.

But he stopped, tore his mouth from hers, and she shuddered at the sensual loss. He stripped the blanket from her shoulders, strode over and spread it out beside the fire. Then he turned to face her again.

She gazed at him in the flickering firelight, at his tall, muscled body tightened with hunger, his eyes glittering in his dangerous face. His shirt hung open, revealing his sculpted chest and the hard, flat line of his waist. She swallowed with effort, desperate to touch his heated skin, to feel those muscles flex under her palms.

He reached out his hand, and she went to him. He pulled her tightly against him, setting off an explosion of need in her blood. He drew his hands up her naked thighs, cupped her bare bottom beneath her shirt, sending thrills chasing over her skin. Then he tugged her even closer, fitting her to his growing arousal, and fused his mouth to hers. It was like coming home, a heady sensation she couldn't resist—feeling cherished, wanted, desired. And every part of her rejoiced.

She sank deeper into the kiss, her world spinning. His hands continued their erotic assault. Her body moistened, craving him with an urgency she couldn't contain. A whimper escaped her throat.

He moved his mouth to her jaw, over the sensitive skin of her neck. She dropped her head back to grant him access, the feverish jolts scorching her skin.

"I need to see you," he muttered against her throat. "Take off the shirt."

She fumbled with the buttons, but couldn't undo them. She gave up, tore it open. Deven leaned back to give her space, and the fabric slid down her arms.

His ravenous eyes tracked the movement. His Adam's apple dipped in his throat. And then his gaze devoured her, making a hot, leisurely slide over every inch of her naked skin. Her legs weakened with need.

A slight breeze puckered her nipples, drawing goose bumps on her skin. She shivered, started to cross her arms, but he grabbed them and held them apart. His gaze made another deliberate trek over her body, and then his hot mouth went to her breast.

She gasped at the fierce zap of pleasure. Tremors buffeted her in waves. She couldn't think, could only reel from the erotic sensations, never wanting them to end.

But an eternity later he stopped and lowered her to the blanket. He stripped off his own clothes and tossed them aside. Her breath caught at the sight of him. He was glorious, riveting, all roped muscles and rigid flesh. The glimmering firelight gilded his skin.

He knelt beside her, urging her back against the blanket, and covered her body with his. Her breath came too fast. The feel of his hard, male body ignited hers.

He kissed her again, his mouth turning urgent. His hands roamed her belly, her breasts. A delicious ache drove out every thought, and she gave herself up to the bliss.

But instead of hurrying to completion, he slowed. He ran his mouth down her throat, her breasts, her thighs, worshipping her body, as if consumed by the moment. The exquisite torture drove her out of her mind.

This was what she'd remembered. The fury of the sensual onslaught. The torment of his languid retreat. The way he'd teased her, excited her with ruthless mastery, building the pleasure until she'd wanted to scream.

She plunged her hands in his short, silky hair, thrilling to the erotic scrape of his jaw. His hands stroked everywhere except where she needed him most, and her frustration built.

When she tugged on his shoulders, he made a low, sexy laugh, then moved back up. For an eternity he stayed poised above her, his face tense with hunger, his eyes hot with desire. And the sheer beauty of the moment struck her, this sharing of body and hearts.

His gaze dipped, and he fingered the borrowed necklace. He closed his eyes, as if unable to bear the sight, then looked at her with such naked yearning that a deep ache seized her chest. And waves of emotions flooded through her. Tenderness. Longing.

Love.

"Maya," he pleaded, his voice hoarse.

And then he entered her, thick and full and hard, and

the pleasure came in deep, rolling waves. She was lost in the ecstasy, unable to think, to stop. The feelings crested, splintered inside her.

"Maya," he cried again. And then he kissed her, swallowing her frantic whimpers, and drove them over the edge.

He shuddered against her mouth, continued the erotic assault. Her body soared out of control. And then the world stopped twirling and the bliss began to ebb.

Long moments later, he withdrew, then eased to the side, pulling her with him. With one arm firmly around her, he pulled the blanket over them both and closed his eyes.

She sighed, nestled her cheek in the hollow of his shoulder, felt the strong, vibrant beat of his heart. Aftermaths of pleasure still skidded through her veins.

For an eternity, she snuggled against him. The soft glow of the fire, the warmth of his muscled arms cocooned her, sheltering her from the darkness, driving out thoughts of the danger ahead. But as the rapture slowly subsided, reality crept back.

This interlude had changed nothing.

She exhaled and forced herself to face facts. She didn't regret what they'd done. They'd shared their bodies, fulfilled a basic human need, forged a memory that would always endure.

And maybe they'd both healed a bit from the painful past.

But nothing had really changed between them. There was still much about him she didn't know, things he refused to confide.

Things somehow wrapped up with Singh and her medallion.

She raised her head and gazed at Deven's handsome face. His stubbled cheeks were relaxed in sleep, the lines on his forehead less pronounced. She traced the long scar bolting across his cheek, admired the noble line of his nose.

No matter what Deven believed, he was a decent man. She had no doubts about that. But he had a darkness inside him now, a terrible secret he wouldn't reveal.

And somehow, before this journey was over, she would discover what it was.

But she had to be careful. She had a real weakness for this man; he affected her as no one else ever had. She had to protect herself, not repeat her mistakes. She'd barely recovered before.

And she definitely shouldn't let herself fall in love with him again.

But as she closed her eyes, the wonderful sensations he'd evoked still pulsing in her veins, she knew that she'd never stopped.

Chapter 9

Making love to Maya ranked right up there as one of the dumbest things he'd ever done.

Deven headed back down the trail he'd discovered, disgusted by his lack of control. He'd had no right to touch her. He'd succumbed in a moment of weakness, given in to the rampaging need.

And the hot, sultry feel of her... He paused and closed his eyes at the onslaught of memories—her ripe, naked breasts; her satin hair pooling over his skin; her erotic, throaty cries.

He opened his eyes, continued hiking down the path. She'd felt right, absolutely perfect in his arms, as if she belonged there. As if she were *his*—just as she had been twelve years ago when she'd given her virginity to him.

And even knowing it was wrong, he craved her again. He wanted to go to her, strip the clothes from her glorious body and sheath himself in her warmth. To plunge into her again and again until her eyes grew glazed and her body shuddered with his.

He exhaled, his blood running heavy and thick, and firmly suppressed the unruly need. He'd screwed up, indulged where he'd had no business. And now he had to apologize—and make sure it didn't happen again, for her own good.

Maya emerged from the cave as he approached. And before he could stop it, his gaze helplessly roamed every inch of her—her curving hips, her graceful arms, the fullness of her breasts. She'd braided her hair, emphasizing the elegant cast of her cheekbones and those bewitching, dark-lashed eyes. She was a sensual fantasy, all soft, satin skin and tempting heat.

A fantasy that could never be his. Because when she learned the entire truth about him…

He stopped near her, not sure what to say. "Maya, listen. Last night, I—"

"Deven, don't." She held up her hand to ward him off. "Please. Let's not talk about it, all right?"

Knocked off stride, he frowned. "You want to pretend it didn't happen?"

"No, of course not." Her face turned pink. "Last night was…wonderful, amazing."

Amazing was right. Blood rushed to his loins at the thought.

"But let's not start complicating things, all right? Let's not apologize. Just…let it go."

"No apologies." His scowl deepening, he planted his hands on his hips. He knew he should feel relieved. She was keeping the encounter casual, offering him the perfect way out.

But something didn't ring true here. He didn't believe her nonchalance. He studied the determined line of her mouth, the way her gaze didn't quite meet his.

And awareness struck him with the force of a bullet. She was acting out of self-defense. She expected *him* to reject *her*. And why shouldn't she? After the last time they'd made love, he'd walked away.

He gripped the back of his neck, sick with self-disgust. He felt like the worst kind of heel.

But she'd pegged him right. He was backing away. They had no future together, and he couldn't touch her again.

And maybe he should allow her the pretense of indifference, let her cling to her ravaged pride. It might be kinder that way. But damned if he could let her think he didn't care.

He stepped close, so close she had to lift her chin to meet his eyes. "But just so you know," he said, unable to hide the desire roughening his voice, "I wish I could give you more. You deserve more." She deserved marriage, children… But he could never marry her. And he couldn't tell her why. She wouldn't trust him if she knew.

And he couldn't bear her disgust.

"I don't want anything else," she said, the false bravado in her voice making his chest ache. "So let's just forget it."

He shook his head, his eyes still holding hers. "I'll remember last night until the day I die."

She flushed again, deeper this time, and his own pulse surged in response. He fisted his hands, wrestling with the urge to yank her into his arms and show her with excruciating thoroughness every erotic detail etched in his mind.

But a deep *whop, whop, whop* rose in the distance, and he dragged his gaze away. He scanned the pine trees towering above them, searched the patches of early-dawn sky.

"A helicopter," she said, fear creeping into her voice.

"Yeah." A Huey. The cadence of the rotors gave it away. "Get into the cave."

He strode to the fire ring, made sure no lingering smoke

would give them away, then followed her inside. He stopped just past the entrance and peered out.

Maya hovered at his elbow. The noise of the rotors grew. "Do you think they can see us?"

"No, the trees are too thick. I doubt they'll even spot the cave."

"But what if they do?"

Tension coiled inside him, but he forced his voice to stay calm. "We'll be gone by the time they find a place to land."

In reality, the Huey didn't need to land. A door gunner could fire from the air, or a man could rappel to the ground. But he didn't intend to worry her about that.

The noise intensified, thundering through the musty cave and vibrating the soles of his feet. Then the nearby trees thrashed from the downdraft, and Deven's eyes confirmed what he already knew. It was a Huey, all right—a military gunship.

And it appeared to be hunting them.

But whose was it? Interpol had access to Hueys and so did Magnum, but they couldn't be trying to rescue him, since they didn't know where he'd gone.

Singh knew he was out here—but where had he gotten a Huey? Romanistan's military didn't own one, and neither did the various terrorist groups he supported—as far as Deven knew.

The helicopter hovered, swaying above the pine trees, its deafening noise blasting his ears. Then the deep, rapid whomping receded as it moved off. Silence descended again.

And Deven turned his mind to his most pressing problem— getting Maya away from here fast.

He caught her worried gaze. "I found a trail earlier," he told her. "It's washed out in spots, but we can get through. It probably leads to a village where we can get supplies and find out where we are."

"But what about the helicopter? Won't it come back?"

"I doubt it. They have a lot of area to check. And even if they do, the trees are thick."

She nodded, but the tension in her eyes didn't ease.

Wanting to reassure her, he reached out, cradled her soft cheek. "Don't worry. We're going to be fine."

She lifted her chin, a determined glint entering her eyes. "I know."

A warm feeling curled around his heart. This was the woman he remembered, the crusader brave enough to take on Singh. And despite his vow to resist her, despite knowing that he shouldn't touch her, he leaned down and took her mouth. He only meant to reassure her, but as his lips slid over hers, as the scent of her skin, the seductive heat of her mouth made his pulse began to thump, he knew that he was doomed. This woman was a need in his blood, a hunger he couldn't sate.

And as she sank into the kiss, her body responding to his, he knew she felt it, too. It took all his strength to pull away.

But they didn't have time to waste. "We'd better go."

"Right." She managed another tight smile, and his respect for her grew. She was a fighter, all right. Now he had to keep this courageous woman safe.

"I'll lead." He picked up the blanket containing the supplies they'd culled—the remaining food, a bottle of water—and swung it over his back. "All set?"

She nodded, and he strode from the cave, casting an uneasy glance at the sky—because despite what he'd told Maya, he was worried about this trek. The police would keep combing the hills. That chopper patrolled overhead. And if Singh had found Maya's drawing—if he'd forced that bookseller to talk before he'd killed him—he might have realized they would head to the monastery and be setting a trap.

And if that weren't bad enough, he was mired in his own personal hell, yearning for a woman he couldn't have.

He waited for Maya to catch up, then led the way up the narrow path, alert for signs of pursuit. Pine needles muffled his steps. The crisp morning air cooled his arms.

And his resolve hardened with every stride. No matter how hard it was to resist her, he couldn't touch Maya again. He'd surrendered to a moment of weakness, but now he had to clamp down, exert control and concentrate on bringing down Singh.

And then get himself out of her life.

Before he lost every shred of decency he'd once possessed and begged her to love him again.

Maya was a wreck.

It was bad enough that the helicopter dogged their steps. All day long it had thundered in and out of view, the ominous drum of its rotors sending them fleeing for cover in the steep terrain.

It was worse that she now had to rethink the past twelve years, that everything she'd believed about Deven's departure was wrong.

But that one blunt statement had unraveled her completely, putting her so on edge she could hardly think.

"I'll remember last night until the day I die."

His words echoed through her mind as they had all day, sparking another flurry of excitement in her veins. She followed him up the steep, narrow path, trying to keep up with his powerful strides. And her mind kept leaping to his deep voice rumbling in the dark, the addictive scent of his skin.

She pressed her hand to her chest to quiet her heart. She was a disaster, all right. Instead of watching the trail, she kept admiring his body. Instead of listening for their pursuers, she kept hearing those intimate words. And instead of trying to figure out the mystery of her medallion, she kept reliving every second of that blissful night, battling the urge to launch herself into his arms.

She exhaled again, heavier this time, knowing she had to get a grip. No matter how much she ached to touch him again, no matter how tempted she was to surrender to the hunger stirring her blood, she had to concentrate on surviving this mess.

The police had to know where they were by now. Why else was that helicopter buzzing the trail? And she knew what Deven was thinking; she'd seen the grim set of his mouth. He feared that Singh's men would be at the monastery, lying in wait.

And it made sense. The monastery was a well-known way station for travelers, a historical shelter for refugees. Once the police had spotted them at that roadblock, they had to know where they'd gone.

She glanced at the sun-dappled trail ahead and realized Deven had disappeared. She hiked past a clump of rhododendrons, rounded a boulder jutting into the path, then spotted him several yards ahead at the crest of the hill.

He turned his head at her approach and raised his finger to his lips. She straggled to a stop behind him, braced her hands on her knees and struggled to catch her breath. "What…is it?"

"The monastery." He shifted to the side, giving her room to see around him. She wiped her forehead on her sleeve, straightened, then took in the breathtaking view.

The monastery clung to the sheer mountain cliffs at the end

of a narrow valley. The snow-covered peaks of Mount Sangkat towered behind it. Steep, rocky ravines plunged down either side. A massive rampart encircled the turreted buildings, like a medieval fortress, as if the forbidding mountains weren't enough to keep intruders out.

The monastery was magnificent, formidable, impassible—except through the lone gate in the center of the high stone wall.

Peering closer, she spotted men standing at intervals along the rampart, and her stomach plunged. *Guards.*

"Who do you think put those guards there?"

"Singh."

"But why would he take over the monastery?"

"To hunt for us. Or force information from the monks."

Swallowing hard, she scanned the guarded wall, the cliffs, the jagged ravines plummeting down the sides. A dirt road stretched from the monastery across the open valley to the village below where they stood.

She eyed the crude wooden huts of the village, the chickens pecking the mud. Then she traced the road back through the valley to the gate. It was the only way inside.

"What are we going to do?"

"Good question." Deven rubbed his hand over his face.

Maya dragged her gaze from Deven's profile to the handful of farmers working the fields. They couldn't just waltz through the gate, not if those guards belonged to Singh. But they hadn't traveled all this way only to be locked out.

Without warning, deep, rhythmic vibrations filled the air. Another spurt of fear spiked her throat. "The helicopter."

"Come on." He grasped her arm, pulled her back down the trail with him into the woods.

He dropped her arm when he reached a thicket, then shoved his way inside. She plunged in after, ignoring the sharp twigs stabbing her scalp. She dove to the ground beside him, landing in a carpet of leaves.

The rapid whomp of rotors grew louder. Reverberations shook the ground. Deven threw his arm around her shoulders, and she huddled against him, not daring to move.

The helicopter came closer, the roar thundering through her skull. She clamped her hands over her ears, curled tighter into a ball, praying they couldn't be seen from the air.

Then suddenly, a shadow moved over the woods. She looked up through the leaves, saw three sinister helicopters pass overhead.

Her mouth turned to dust. Exactly who were they fighting here?

The vibrations rattled her bones, her teeth. The bushes around them thrashed. Just when she feared they'd been detected, the noise began to recede.

Long seconds later, she pressed her sweating palms to her knees. "What was that?" She couldn't keep the horror from her voice.

"I'm not sure."

"Was it the military? The police?"

Deven gave his head a shake. "Romanistan doesn't own any Hueys. Someone else must be working with Singh."

"Someone else?" She'd known Singh had influence beyond the borders, but to have foreign forces patrolling the sky... How could they possibly fight that?

Deven shoved his way out of the thicket, then held the branches aside. She crawled out and stumbled behind him up the hill.

Still shaken by the sight of those choppers, she studied the valley again. Farmers toiled in the fields. A peasant trudged toward the monastery's gate, carting a monstrous load of straw on her back.

"We have to go through that gate," Deven said.

She'd come to the same conclusion. "But how?"

"We'll have to disguise ourselves as villagers. They're the only ones going inside."

She eyed the dirt track snaking through the valley, the peasants plodding along. He was right. Still…

"It would be better if I go in alone," he said carefully. "We'd be less noticeable that way."

"Forget it. We had a deal, remember? The medallion stays with me."

"The deal was that I'd keep you safe." He folded his muscled arms.

Their gazes met—and dueled. His mouth formed an unyielding line.

And she realized that he wasn't just acting stubborn; he was trying to protect her. She forced herself to gentle her voice. "Look, Deven. I know what you're trying to do, and I appreciate it. I do. But I'm not that fragile. I'm the Leopard. I sneak around all the time. You don't have to worry about me."

"This is different. We don't know what we'll find in there."

"So? I've taken on Singh before." And Deven knew that. He'd found in her in Singh's palace. So why was he balking now?

Frowning, she thought back to the first night she'd seen him, to his dire warnings about probing the past. And suddenly she understood. He wasn't only trying to protect her from Singh. He feared what she might learn about her medallion—and herself.

She clasped the chain around her neck, sobered by the thought. All her life, she had fantasized about this medallion, imagining it to be something good—that it protected her, that someone kind had given it to her, that it came from her lost family as a token of love.

But what if it wasn't so good? What if it was related to something sinister, something evil? What if she didn't like what she found?

Deven's gaze swerved back to hers. And in those dark depths, she saw more than the desire to protect her. She saw concern, sympathy.

And another realization blasted through her. Deven understood her dilemma. He'd hinted at discoveries he'd made about his own past—things too terrible to reveal. Now he wanted to spare her that pain.

She rested her hand on his muscled forearm, struck again by his concern. How could this man believe he wasn't good?

"It's my medallion," she said softly. "My past. Whatever meaning it has—even if it's a bad one—I need to know."

His eyes stayed on hers for several heartbeats. And then he inclined his head, respect mingling with understanding in his eyes. "Fair enough."

He turned his attention to the valley again. "Think you can carry a load of straw that far?"

She scanned the distance from the village to the gate—at least a couple of miles. She tried to keep the doubt from her voice. "If I have to."

"It's the best way to hide your face."

She shifted her gaze to the woman still hobbling along the trail—carrying a load so huge that the straw appeared to have legs.

And she had to admit the disguise would work—as long as she didn't collapse. "All right. Straw it is."

But as they crept down the mountain into the village, the terrible irony struck her. She'd finally managed to stop thinking about Deven and get her mind off the previous night. But now a far worse worry consumed her—what she might discover about herself inside those walls.

Chapter 10

He should have forced her to stay behind.

Deven paused on the dirt road leading to the monastery, unable to stem a feeling of impending doom. He shifted his unwieldy bundle of straw, adjusted the leather head strap that secured the load to his back, then peered at the monastery again. Its rampart loomed twenty feet above him—impenetrable, unyielding, as formidable as the sheer granite cliffs slashing the sky. Along the top of the wall stood guards armed with semiautomatic weapons—guards wearing the black uniform of Singh's men.

Another feeling of dread slithered through him, that fear that he couldn't quite shake—fear that he was leading Maya toward something evil. Fear that he'd fail to protect her, that whatever they'd find behind those walls would forever change their lives.

His jaw rigid with tension, he waited while she staggered up the trail behind him, doubled over beneath her enormous pile of straw. Only her dusty pants were visible beneath the massive load—which was the point of the disguise.

But she had to be in agony. Scratchy straw rained over her head. That load weighed at least sixty pounds. The two-mile hike probably felt like twenty by now—especially given her strenuous trek all day and the little sleep she'd had last night.

But she hadn't complained. She'd even taken the sight of Singh's men in stride. She was brave, determined—and she was right. She deserved to know the meaning of her medallion.

Even if his instincts screamed at him to haul her away from the danger fast.

"We're almost there," he said when she'd caught up. "Only another fifty feet. Remember not to stop no matter what."

"I know." Her voice came out muffled beneath the straw.

Blinking away the sweat stinging his eyes, he shifted his own brutal load and continued toward the gate. He scanned the late-afternoon shadows creeping out from the wall, the blood-black slashes of the steep ravines. Singh's helicopters rumbled ominously in the distance, like a monster growling deep in the earth.

He passed beneath the thick, arched gateway, felt the scrutiny of Singh's men. He kept his head down, his pace slow, but his mind raced with impressions and plans. That medallion *had* to be important. Singh would never have gone to this extent merely to capture them.

Now they had to ditch their loads, find the head monk and ask about the inscription—and make sure they didn't get trapped.

He veered around the monastery's central courtyard, following the directions of the farmer who'd sold him the straw. Prayer bells chimed in the distance. The sound of trickling water indicated a fountain nearby. He trudged through the deepening shadows, moving slowly enough that Maya didn't lag behind.

The bleating of a goat confirmed that he was nearing the stable. The gurgling water sounded closer, along with the chanting of monks at prayer. When he reached the stable, he paused, scanned the buildings around the courtyard to orient himself, and eyed the man standing guard at the door.

"Dump the straw over there," the guard ordered, pointing to a mound of straw inside the stable. "And be quick about it."

Mumbling agreement, Deven plodded past the guard, then stopped before the pile of straw. He heaved the load off his back, wiped his sweaty face on his sleeve and took a quick glance around the enclosed yard.

A young, red-robed monk tended goats at the back of the stable. Only the one man guarded the door—but he had a machine gun slung over his back, and probably more weapons tucked out of sight.

Then Maya staggered over, and he reached for the straw on her back. "Hold up," he said, knowing she couldn't see much. He lifted the load off her back, and she instantly sank to the ground.

"My back," she groaned. "Oh, God. I think it's wrecked for life."

Grunting in sympathy, he tossed her bundle on the pile, then blinked back the dust from his eyes. He wished he could let her rest. But every second they spent here endangered them more.

He glanced at the monk tending the goats, then back to the surly guard. "I'm going to call him over," he told her under his breath. He tugged out his gun, positioning it so the guard wouldn't see. "Keep your head down and don't get up. Act sick. I'm going to knock him out."

"Be careful," she whispered. She lowered her head to the ground and groaned.

Keeping his back bent to hide his face, he motioned to the guard. "Hello," he called out in the local dialect. "We have a problem."

The guard turned to him and scowled. "What is it?"

"My wife. She can't get up." Maya let out another groan.

"Kick her," the guard said. "Then hurry up and get out."

"I tried that, but she won't move." Deven bent over Maya, his pulse accelerating as the guard stomped toward them, muttering about villagers too lazy to work. The thud of his boots grew louder. The guard moved into Deven's peripheral vision and stopped.

"What's the matter?"

"She's sick. If you help me lift her, I can carry her out."

"The hell I will." As Deven expected, the guard turned toward the young monk working nearby. "Hey, you! Get over here and pick this woman up."

Before the guard could turn back, Deven wheeled around, slammed the butt of his gun into his neck. The guard grunted, swayed. Deven hit him again, and he fell to the stable floor.

"Rip your scarf into thirds," Deven told Maya. "I need it to tie him up."

She jumped to her feet. "Do you have a knife?"

He dug in his pocket and tossed her his penknife. While she slashed at her scarf, he grabbed the guard's ankles and dragged him behind the tall stacks of straw. Using the sections of cloth Maya gave him, he bound the guard's hands and feet and gagged his mouth. Then he swung the guard's machine gun over his back and tucked his pistol and extra clips into his pants. He kept his own gun firmly in hand. "All right. Let's go."

Fully armed now, he rose and glanced at the young monk cowering behind the braying goats. "Where's the head monk, the abbot?" Deven asked. "We need to talk to him."

The monk straightened, but his face was pale, his dark eyes wide with fear. He glanced around the stable, shifted his weight from foot to foot, as if preparing to bolt.

"We're not going to hurt you," Maya said quickly. "We're not with these men. We've come to talk to the abbot."

"We need information," Deven added. "That's all. Don't be afraid."

The young monk glanced at the guard on the ground, then back to them. His gaze stalled on Deven's guns. "You...you can't see him. He was attacked last night."

Oh, hell. "He's dead?"

"Not yet, but they say he won't last the day."

"What happened?"

The monk shook his shaved head. "I'm not sure. I only know that these men came in, and now they won't let anyone leave."

Maya stepped forward. "Please, we have to see him. It's urgent, and we've come a long way. At least tell us where he is so we can try."

The monk's eyes flicked from Maya to him, and then he motioned with one scrawny arm. "He's in the protector chapel beside the library. The third door down."

"Who's with him?" Deven asked.

"Another monk. He's meditating with him."

"How many guards?"

"Only the one at the door."

Deven turned toward Maya, knowing they had to act fast. The guards could spot them at any time. "Ready?"

"Yes."

Motioning for her to follow, he strode across the stable to the door. He peeked out at the low buildings surrounding the courtyard, the late-afternoon shadows darkening the paths. A dozen guards had clustered near the gate, gambling. Good. They'd be too busy placing bets to notice them.

He swept his gaze in the other direction, to the small red porch by the chapel door. An armed guard paced past.

Deven leaned toward Maya. "We'll do this in stages. As soon as the guard turns away, run to the next doorway. I'll be right behind you."

"All right." Her brows wrinkled in concentration. He took hold of her arm, his tension rising as the guard paced toward them again. The guard turned.

"Go," Deven whispered, and released her arm.

Maya darted forward, and he followed, their steps soundless as they rushed to the door. They slipped into the recessed alcove, their soft pants mingling in the cooling air.

Signaling for her to wait, he eyed the men milling around the gate again, then fastened his gaze on the pacing guard. Cooking pots clanged in the room behind him. The smell of curry made his stomach growl.

"Get ready," he whispered. The guard completed his rotation and turned. "Now."

He waited a beat, then raced behind her to the next doorway and once again scooted inside. Breathing hard now, he glanced back at the gate, scanned the still-empty courtyard. The rhythmic murmur of chanting filled the air.

Only one more building to go.

But the next one would be the trickiest. He needed to divert the guard's attention, get him to move farther away from the porch so they had time to get through the door.

"Hold on," he said. He checked the ground around his feet,

scooped up some pebbles, then eyed the small porch again, gauging the time they'd need to run.

He knew he was taking a gamble. By creating a distraction, he might raise the guard's suspicions and prompt him to mount a search. And if he found the bound guard...

But better to risk that than engage in a gun battle now.

"All right, get ready." He held his breath, waited until the guard paced past the chapel's porch. Then he sprang into action and hurled the stones into the shadows past the guard. The pebbles plopped in the dirt; the guard jerked up his head, then rushed to investigate the sound.

"Run," Deven said.

Maya dashed to the porch, leaped up the steps and slipped inside. His eyes glued on the guard, Deven followed her into the chapel and shut the door.

They'd made it—but the room unsettled him even more. He eyed the dozens of flickering candles, the bloodred pillars painted with symbols, the warlike masks scowling from the walls. Stuffed wolves snarled from tables and corners, their sharp teeth gleaming in the light.

"What is this place?" He waved a cloud of pungent incense from his eyes.

"I don't know." She moved closer, not that Deven blamed her. He frowned at the savage wolves, the grimacing masks. The odd room made his skin crawl, intensifying his instinct to whisk her away.

Then a movement in the shadows stirred the smoke. He pulled Maya behind him and raised his gun. But a monk emerged, his head shaved, his red robes swirling around his bare feet. He caught sight of them and stopped.

Deven lowered his weapon. "We need to talk to the abbot."

The monk eyed the machine gun slung over his shoulder,

the pistol Deven still held in his hand. His eyes widened, but he planted his feet and crossed his arms. "They're chanting the death prayers now. He can't be disturbed. He must be left alone to prepare."

"Please," Maya pleaded, stepping out from behind him. "It's urgent. We need to talk to him about the inscription on my medallion." She tugged it from beneath her tunic and held it up. The silver piece gleamed in the candlelight.

The monk glanced at the medallion, blinked, then leaned closer for a better look. His jaw turned slack. He shook his head, as if in disbelief. Then he bowed, began to back up. "Yes. Of course. This way. The abbot is expecting you."

Expecting them? Deven shot a glance at Maya. She shrugged back, looking equally as confused. Hoping this wasn't a trap, that Singh wasn't lying in wait, he kept his gun ready as he followed the monk.

They walked down a long, narrow hallway, the stone floor worn with age, faded prayer flags strung over the walls. More masks and wolves with their fangs bared glowered at them from every side, putting him on edge. When they reached a room at the end of the hall, the monk stepped aside and motioned for them to go in.

Deven slipped off his shoes as a sign of respect and entered first. His gaze arrowed straight to the man lying on a narrow cot. The abbot's eyes were closed, his head swathed in bandages. Burning candles surrounded the bed. Another monk wearing a red robe and white headband knelt on the floor by the abbot's side, chanting and ringing a bell.

There was a golden statue of Buddha in the corner, religious murals decorating the walls. Sticks of yellow incense smoldered nearby, the thick smoke choking the air.

Stepping closer to the cot, he eyed the abbot's pallid face, heard his faint breath rattle and wheeze, and his hopes plunged. The young monk in the stable was right. The abbot wouldn't last the day.

The kneeling monk stopped chanting, then rose and stepped away from the bed. Maya quickly took his place. *"Namaste,"* she said in greeting, raising her hands in respect.

The abbot stirred and opened his eyes. "Is it you?" he whispered.

She shot Deven a questioning frown, then knelt beside the bed. "We've come for help," she told the abbot, pulling the medallion from around her neck. "I've had this charm since I was a child. I don't know where it came from. But there's something written on the back in a language we don't understand, and we hoped that you could help."

The abbot stretched out his bare, bony arm, and Maya placed the medallion in his trembling hand. He brought it close to his face, peered at it for several seconds, his hooded eyes unreadable in the shifting light.

Then, to Deven's surprise, he kissed it and closed his eyes. "I knew you would come," he wheezed. "I saw the signs. It was foretold that in my lifetime…"

Frowning, Deven moved closer to hear his faint words, wondering if the abbot was delirious with pain. "Can you tell us anything about the inscription, what it says?"

"Yes." The abbot opened his eyes and reverently traced the inscription. "It's written in Abatta, a language spoken here until the eleventh century."

So they'd been right. Deven held his breath.

The abbot turned the medallion over, studied the figure of Parvati on the front. "It was made at the ancient temple, home of the Hindu cult of Parvati."

"How can you tell?" Maya asked.

"Her sacred thread, her bare breasts…those are ancient signs of her divinity." He coughed, then dragged in a reedy breath.

"Parvati is the mother goddess…*She of the mountains*… daughter of the Himalayas. The crescent moon is for Shiva, her consort."

The abbot wheezed, gurgled, and Deven tensed. The other monk hurried over with a cup of water, but the abbot refused his help.

"The king commissioned the medallion when the Muslims invaded," the abbot continued. "Soon after that, the cult was destroyed."

Deven went still. If the medallion was connected to the Muslim invasion… Excitement poured through him. This couldn't be a coincidence. Singh had to be hunting for the crown, the last missing treasure from the Roma legend—a fact that might link him to the Order of the Black Crescent Moon.

The abbot closed his eyes, his voice fading. "A few holy men survived. Later, they built this monastery…"

He didn't speak for several seconds, and Deven waited, his pulse pounding his veins. Had he passed out? Would they be left without the rest of the information when they had come so close?

But then the abbot opened his glazed eyes. "Things changed over the centuries. We're a Buddhist monastery now. But we have guarded the sacred knowledge, passed it from head monk to head monk…waiting for you."

"For me?" Maya's shocked voice filled the room.

"Waiting for the medallion," the abbot clarified, handing it back to her. "Now you must find the sadhu hermit living in the Forbidden Valley. He will tell you the rest."

A sadhu? He had to be kidding. With Singh on their tail, they didn't have time for detours—especially to chase down one of the ash-covered ascetics who'd renounced worldly life.

But the abbot hadn't finished. He signaled to the monk. "Bring her the box."

The monk took a small, ornately carved box from a table and carried it over. Deven studied the box, and a sudden whisper of menace coursed through him. Stepping closer to Maya, he placed a protective hand on her shoulder. It took all his willpower not to yank her away, to shield her from a danger he could sense but not see.

"Open it," the abbot said.

Maya lifted the lid. Inside was a small scrolled parchment tied with a golden thread. She pulled it out and handed it to the dying man.

"No, you keep it," he said. "It's a map to the sadhu's cave. You must hurry, arrive before the lunar eclipse. Only one day left... It was foretold." He raised his hands, pressed them together in a gesture of respect to Maya, stunning Deven even more.

"But the inscription! What... Oh, no," Maya cried as the abbot slumped back against the cot.

The monk hurried over and shooed them aside. "He needs to meditate, to prepare. Please, you must go now."

"Go?" Deven protested. "But we don't have answers."

"I'm sorry," the monk said. "There isn't time."

Maya hung the medallion around her neck, tucked the scroll into her pocket and rose. Filled with frustration, Deven watched her make her own sign of respect to the abbot, and then he followed her into the hall.

"That was confusing," she said as they slipped into their shoes.

"No kidding." They still didn't have hard answers, just more vague clues. And now they had to travel to the Forbidden Valley, the Bermuda Triangle of the Himalayas—the last place he wanted to go.

Scowling, he eyed the waiting monk. "Who attacked the abbot?"

"The same men who are here now. They came yesterday," the monk added as he led them back down the hall. "They demanded that he explain a drawing, but he wouldn't talk."

Deven's heart tripped. He glanced back at Maya, saw the stunned fear in her eyes. So Singh really had found their paper in the bookstore. Now, thanks to their mistake, the abbot could die.

And Singh was on the trail to that crown.

"Wait! Please!" The monk who'd been praying with the abbot ran behind them, his red robes flapping around his ankles as he rushed to catch up. "The abbot wants to talk to you again," he told Maya, sounding breathless.

Maya shot Deven a questioning look. "Go ahead," he said. "I'll wait."

"All right." She followed the beckoning monk.

Still frowning over their predicament, Deven turned to the other man. "I need to send a message. Are you allowed to use a phone?"

The monk angled his shaved head. "Yes, but we don't have one here. I can call from the market tomorrow—they'll have to let us leave to get food."

"Good. If you have paper, I'll write it down."

The monk led him to a small lacquered table farther down the hallway, then slid open a drawer containing paper and pens. Deven scribbled out a message to his Magnum boss requesting backup, adding that Singh had helicopters patrolling nearby. He scribbled his code phrase—treachery abounds—and put the phone number on the back.

"Call this number," he told the monk. "And read this message exactly as I wrote it." His boss would need that code phrase to verify him. "Then destroy it. That's all you need to do. And don't show it to anyone."

"I understand." He tucked it into his robe.

Deven hesitated, wondering if he should have the monk contact his Interpol boss, but decided against it. His Magnum boss, Skinner, would take care of that.

He wished he could leave Maya with the monks or somewhere safer. The thought of taking her into the Forbidden Valley—where any number of dangers awaited—chilled his blood. But he didn't dare let her out of his sight with Singh's men so close.

She rejoined him then, her dark eyes troubled, a frown marring her smooth face. "What did the abbot want?" he asked.

She shook her head, looking perplexed. "He just mumbled about the danger and the eclipse. It didn't make much sense. I don't think he's quite—"

A shout came from the courtyard, interrupting her words. A burst of semiautomatic gunfire followed, and Deven's adrenaline surged. *Damn*. Singh's men must have discovered the tied-up guard.

He turned to the wild-eyed monk. "Is there another way out of here?" There had to be a secret escape route in a place that routinely sheltered refugees.

The monk shook himself out of his daze. "Yes—the bolt-hole. This way!"

They raced after the monk through the dimly lit hallway, leaped up a short flight of stairs. The monk stopped before a tall, carved chest. "It's behind this."

Deven strode around the chest and grabbed the side, then helped drag it away from the wall. The monk scooted behind it, slid his hands over the wooden panels covering the wall. "The tunnel is low at the start, but it gets better as you go. The door is here somewhere…." He pushed at the spots where the panels joined.

More shots rang out. Tortured screams filled the air. Maya glanced nervously around the hallway, and his own sense of urgency swelled. The need to rush out and defend the monks burned through him. But he had to keep Maya—and that medallion—safe.

Then the panel sprang open, revealing a crudely chiseled tunnel about shoulder high. Dank, musty air wafted out.

"There are torches—flashlights—just inside," the monk said. "And a basket with other supplies. Take everything with you and follow the tunnel to the end. It takes about an hour. You'll come out at a river. You can follow the map from there."

"Thank you," Maya said.

The monk nodded, pressed his palms together in farewell.

Deven picked up the flashlights by the door and handed one to Maya. He flicked his on, then entered the frigid tunnel, bending over to accommodate his frame. The weak beam bounced off the rocks.

Maya stepped inside, and then the door clicked shut behind them. Still ducking his head, Deven glanced back as best he could. Maya stood clutching her flashlight, her dark eyes huge.

"Are you all right?" he asked, wishing he had room to turn around and hold her.

"Just worried…confused."

"Yeah." That abbot had raised more questions than answers. But they'd mull that over later. Right now they had to escape this place. "We'd better get moving. I don't know how long these batteries will last." He picked up the basket of supplies, tucked it under his arm.

A scraping sound came from outside the tunnel—the monk pushing the chest back into place. It settled against the door with a muffled thud. The sound echoed through the darkness like a knell of doom.

Deven started down the low tunnel, trying to shake the misgivings off. But that growing sense of peril dogged him, that feeling of dread. As if they were heading toward something evil, something deadly, an enemy he couldn't see.

Something he'd better figure out fast—before more innocent people lost their lives.

Chapter 11

Maya plodded behind Deven through the darkness, barely able to stand upright in the narrow space, the earthy air thick in her lungs. They'd inched along for nearly an hour, working their way down a slick, sloping passage, chiseled into the rocks.

Her exhausted legs trembled. Her lower back screamed with pain. She struggled not to think about the damp walls pressing in from every side, the total darkness beyond Deven's dwindling light. Her own flashlight had died long ago.

Deven's machine gun clanked against the wall. His shoes thudded rhythmically against the stones. The faint beam from his flashlight bounced off the rough-hewn rocks, cutting through a silence so profound that it roared.

"Watch out for this step," he called back.

Bracing her hand on the wall, she stopped and saw that the tunnel made another sudden drop. Who knew that walking downhill could be so much work? It took all her concentration to keep from sliding on the angled rocks.

"You all right?" Deven called back.

"Just…catching…my breath." She sucked in the fetid air, realizing she was near collapse—and not just physically. The stress of being on the run for days, the guilt over the abbot's attack, hearing those poor monks scream… She shivered, trying to stifle the lingering fear.

She didn't know what to think about her medallion. In fact, she didn't want to think at all. She wanted to curl into a ball and succumb to the oblivion of sleep.

But she'd never shrunk from her problems before, and she wouldn't do it now—no matter how depleted she felt.

"I can hear the river." Deven's deep voice echoed in the gloom. "We're almost there. We'll rest when we get to the end."

She tipped her head, made out a faint rushing sound above her pounding pulse. Galvanized now that they were close, she maneuvered the step down, then trudged behind Deven again. Water seeped from the ceiling and dripped onto her scalp. The dank odor permeated the air. Her medallion swung against her chest, the solid weight familiar, comforting, as she followed Deven's bobbing light through the dark.

"I still can't believe my medallion is a thousand years old," she said. "It should be in a museum."

"The date's interesting."

"The eleventh century?" She splashed through a ribbon of water and tried to remember Romanistan's medieval history. The Muslims had invaded, of course, just as the abbot had said, and during the ensuing war, the Roma had either fled their homeland or died.

She shuddered at the thought of the slaughter, the dying

people's screams… Like the poor monks they'd just left behind.

"What bothers you about it?" she asked, not wanting to think about the monks.

"The abbot said the king commissioned the medallion."

"So?"

Deven's gun chinked against the stones. "During a war? Doesn't that seem like an odd time to commission a medallion, especially when they'd lost?"

"I don't know. I hadn't thought about it before." She continued following Deven, mulling over his words. But then the sound of running water grew louder, drawing her attention to the passage ahead. The tunnel began to widen. Seconds later, it opened into a chamber, high enough to stand in, big enough to move comfortably around. A pile of rocks blocked the exit. Water rushed past on the other side.

The river. They'd reached the Forbidden Valley. She stumbled to a halt in relief.

Deven set down the basket of supplies and removed his weapons, then stretched his back and groaned. "We might as well spend the night in here. It's too late to hike through the valley now."

"Sounds good to me." She massaged her pulsing forehead, her knees so wobbly she nearly collapsed.

Deven dropped to one knee, pulled a blanket from the basket and tossed it to her. She spread it out, eased herself down and stretched out on the rocky floor.

Her thigh muscles quivered with spasms. Her back and shoulders throbbed. Every inch of her body ached, revealing muscles she never knew she had. And the rock slab felt like heaven. She wanted to roll over and sleep for months.

Unable to move, she rubbed her gritty eyes and watched Deven dig through their supplies. He pulled out a plastic bottle of water and held it up, but she shook her head. He tilted his head back and drank deeply, his Adam's apple dipping in his throat.

And the force of his sexual appeal jolted through her again—the strong, virile lines of his face, the black beard stubble coating his jaw, the sexy hollow at the base of his throat. Her gaze drifted lower, lingering on the dark hair dusting his arms, his lean belly outlined by the cotton shirt, then down to his muscled thighs.

Knowing she was treading on dangerous ground, she turned her mind to the reason they were here—her medallion. "So why would a medieval king commission a medallion?"

Deven screwed the cap on the bottle and wiped his mouth on his sleeve. "Lots of reasons. It could be a medal for bravery in battle. Or something to commemorate an event—a birth, marriage, a battle they'd won."

"But they lost that war.... I doubt they would commemorate that."

Grunting his agreement, he handed her another blanket from the basket, and she spread it over her legs. He propped his flashlight on the ground, and the faint light threw the angles of his face into harsh relief.

She frowned into the gloom beyond the puddle of light, fingered the medallion lying beneath the necklace against her chest. "I don't think this is a medal, either. The abbot said they'd passed on some kind of knowledge. So the medallion must mean something. Something important."

But what? What information would a king need to pass on during a war?

Her mind wandered, conjuring the horror of a medieval war. Enemies charging in on horses. Villages in chaos. Peasants screaming as they tried to flee. She shuddered, knowing the carnage would have been horrendous. Men slain in the roads.

Hysterical mothers clutching their sobbing children and racing into the hills. Families huddling together in terror, hiding from the deadly hordes.

The abbot's words floated through her mind again, and she struggled to connect the thoughts. The Muslims invading. The king commissioning a medallion. Knowledge that they had to pass on. Villagers hiding in the mountains, hiding…

Her heart thudded fast. Her gaze cut to Deven again. "You think the king hid something—something he couldn't take with him during the invasion?"

Deven nodded, his face grim. "I'm almost sure of it."

"Like what? What are you thinking?"

He rose to his feet, paced toward the rocks piled at the entrance, and turned back. "That it's connected to the Roma legend. *The three treasures.* All that happened during the Muslim invasion, and they still haven't found the crown."

She jerked upright, her fatigue abruptly forgotten, electrified by the thought. She'd heard the legend, of course—who hadn't? It was a beloved fairy tale in these parts. According to the tale, the Hindu goddess Parvati, impressed with an eleventh-century king's bravery in battle, rewarded him with three sacred gifts—a necklace, dagger and crown. Together, these treasures gave him the power to rule the world. But Parvati cautioned the king to use those powers wisely—and never for personal gain.

The king obeyed. Decades passed. The Roma prospered and lived in peace.

But then the wise king died, and his impulsive son gained the throne. During the celebration, the newly crowned king watched a beautiful virgin dance. Determined to have her, he misused the powers of the treasures to take her, even though she'd been promised to another man. Devastated and disgraced, the woman cursed the Roma king and condemned his people to roam. A short time later, the Muslims invaded, driving the Roma from their kingdom, and their sacred possessions were lost.

Until recently, no one believed the legend was true, although rumors about the treasures surfaced from time to time. But then, several months ago, the fabled necklace showed up in a Spanish bank vault, part of a cache of forgotten Nazi war loot. Shortly after that, the Roma princess found the sacred dagger buried in an Incan tomb. And now that the world knew the treasures existed, the hunt was on to find the final treasure, the ancient crown.

"You think my medallion leads to the missing crown?"

"It fits. The time frame, the goddess Parvati. The abbot even mentioned the lunar eclipse."

She scrambled to remember the rest of the legend—that when the three sacred gifts were recovered, the curse would be broken and the true Roma leader revealed during a bloodred lunar eclipse.

She shook her head, trying not to let her excitement overrule common sense. "You're saying the king hid the crown, and made this medallion to show its location?"

"It's possible."

"No, it's not. It doesn't make any sense. If the king was going to hide the crown, why didn't he hide the other pieces with it? Why wouldn't he keep them together?"

Deven shrugged. "Who knows? It was a thousand years ago. Maybe he did put them together and they got separated later on. Or maybe he thought the treasures would be safer if he split them up."

"I don't know." She rubbed her throbbing forehead, too tired and confused to think straight. "It sounds so far-fetched."

Deven paced back to the blanket, then lowered himself to the ground. "I know it's a stretch. But Singh could believe it.

And Interpol has been trying to find out if he has ties to the Order of the Black Crescent Moon."

The Order. Her stomach swooped, her world further knocked off-kilter by the thought of the hate-filled group—murderers dedicated to eliminating the Roma worldwide. They'd slaughtered her people for centuries to find the treasures, believing they were the rightful owners.

"Think about it," Deven continued. "That crown is a powerful symbol. If Singh gets it, he could claim to be the rightful king of Romanistan. The people would have to recognize him if he had the crown. And if he gets control of Romanistan's nuclear arsenal…"

Their eyes met. Her hand rose to her throat. *Dear God.* "No one could stop him."

Deven's mouth thinned. His eyes turned black, simmering with anger, determination—and something more.

Her chest tightened with apprehension, along with a terrible feeling of dread. This was far more than a job to him, more than the need to bring down a dangerous man. Deven wanted revenge.

She couldn't blame him. Singh had murdered his mother, driven him away from his country and changed his life. But that feral look in his eyes… A chill penetrated her heart.

Rattled by his reaction, she tugged the medallion from beneath her tunic and held the reassuring weight in her palm. She gazed at the figure of the goddess Parvati, the still-mysterious inscription on the back. Could this possibly be the key to an ancient treasure? It sounded so crazy….

"Supposing we're right," she said slowly, "and this is the key to the missing crown, then how did Singh know about it?"

"I don't know."

And even stranger, how had *she* gotten it? She'd been an

orphan, a street kid, homeless all her life. How had the key to a medieval treasure ended up with her?

Unless it had been stolen.

She grimaced. So much for the fantasy that she'd come from a kind, upstanding family. At best, someone had found the medallion and given it to her, not realizing its worth. And at worst—she was descended from thieves.

Shaking her head at that irony, she watched Deven leap to his feet again and prowl the musty cave. His strong body rippled with energy. His scar formed a somber slash. She eyed the lines bracketing his mouth, those wide shoulders broad enough to protect the world. She'd woven so many dreams around that man—dreams of a family, a home. Love.

She knew better now. Deven would never marry her—no matter how badly she yearned for him, no matter how explosive the sex.

And now she had to put another fantasy to rest—that the medallion signified something good about her past. "I guess we should turn this medallion over to the proper authorities."

Deven pivoted back and braced his hands on his hips. "Not yet. We don't have any facts, just theories. It might not be the key to anything."

"True." The abbot's poor health might have made him delusional. His cryptic warning about danger was proof of that. And even if the medallion was some sort of key, it might lead to something far less exciting than the crown—census records, a philosophical treatise, important to the medieval king and interesting to historians, but hardly a treasure trove.

Plus, who would they give it to? Singh had contacts everywhere. Who could they possibly trust?

She blew out her breath in a sigh. "I guess we need to find that sadhu hermit tomorrow and hear what he has to say. We can decide what to do after that."

Deven strode to the rocks covering the exit and tossed a few aside. Dense bushes sprawled across the opening. The rising wind moaned in the trees.

Without warning, a terrible sense of danger shuddered through her. Maya didn't think she was superstitious, no more than most, but she'd heard stories of the Forbidden Valley for years—a place where people disappeared without a trace, where evil spirits lurked. The wind keened again, and she rubbed her arms.

Deven glanced her way. And she saw that distance in his eyes again, as if he were retreating, blocking her out. "Is something wrong?" she asked.

"No," he said quickly. Too quickly.

She didn't believe him. Something had happened in that monastery today, something that had changed him. He'd been pulling away ever since, becoming even more withdrawn than before.

"I'm going outside to scout around," he said. "You stay here and rest."

"I'm fine. I'll go with you." She got up, stifling a groan as her body ached in protest. She swayed, fought off the dizziness blurring her eyes.

Deven came back to her and gripped her arms. "Maya, you're done in. You hiked all day. You carted that straw for miles. Now you can hardly stand on your feet. Sit back down and rest."

She opened her mouth to argue. Was he that anxious to escape her? Did he think she'd built up expectations about last night? Or worse…was he intending to abandon her here?

She deliberately stifled the doubts. Deven wouldn't do that. Of course, she'd believed that once before….

"No one knows where this tunnel is," he continued. "You'll be safe here. I'll just take a quick look around, then come right back. We'll eat, look at that map, then hike out together at dawn."

She searched his face, saw the sincerity in his eyes. And she realized that somewhere along this journey, she'd come to fully trust him. He might not love her, he still might harbor secrets, but she could rely on him to protect her medallion and her life.

"All right. I'll wait here."

"Good." He brushed her cheek with his calloused hand. His eyes met hers—and held. Awareness shimmered between them, but beyond the desire she saw longing, yearning—the same hunger that ached inside her.

Needing to hold him, she leaned toward him, wanting the comfort and thrill of his touch. But he dropped his hand and stepped back.

She swayed and staggered forward. A sudden ache formed in her throat. She crossed her arms, fighting to beat back the swell of hurt as he turned away.

She hadn't imagined that look. He'd wanted her, and then he'd resisted her. But why? Why erect that wall between them? What could possibly be wrong?

Maybe it was the ordeal they'd been thorough, the utter exhaustion of the past few days. And maybe it was the fact that her world had been turned on end. But she was tired of evasions, tired of secrets. It was past time she got him to talk.

"I'd like to know something, though," she said.

He shoved his pistol into his waistband, then picked up the machine gun, not quite meeting her eyes. "What?"

"I understand why Singh wanted to find your mother, but why is he still after *you?*"

He went dead still. His eyes went blank, his face wooden,

and her stomach jittered with dread. What was so bad that he wouldn't say?

He slowly swung the gun over his back, moving as stiffly as if he'd aged sixty years. Then his gaze returned to hers.

"I told you before, I have something of his, something he wants back. And you know Singh. He never forgives a grudge." His eyes turned stark; his lips curved into a smile so bleak that her belly turned to ice. "But then...neither do I."

He strode to the entrance, tossed several more rocks aside. Then he glanced back, his eyes still tortured. "I'll be back."

"Be careful," she whispered, her mind spinning.

He nodded and slipped through the bushes outside. She sank to the blanket again, her thoughts in total turmoil. What had he taken from Singh? What didn't he want her to know?

She pulled the blanket to her chin and swallowed hard—because the fact that she couldn't answer that question worried her even more.

Maya opened her eyes, disoriented by the total blackness, cold, musty air filling her lungs. Her body throbbed. The sound of flowing water rushed nearby.

The tunnel. The medallion. Deven's revenge against Singh.

Memories of the past two days rushed back, and she pushed herself to sit up, groaning at her aching back. She reached for the flashlight she'd left beside the blanket and clicked it on, but the batteries were dead.

A wolf howled closer to the cave, a long, keening wail that raised goose bumps on her arms. Her mind flashed back to the stuffed wolves in the monastery's chapel, and she shivered hard. What a bizarre sight that had been.

She groped for the basket and pulled it toward her, managing to find a candle and matches at the bottom of the supplies. She scraped a match along the rocks and lit the candle, but the tiny flame did little to dispel the dark. Still uneasy, she dug through the basket for spare batteries, replaced the ones in her flashlight and clicked it on.

The added light helped soothe her nerves—but where was Deven? How much time had passed since he'd left? One hour? Several? The wind moaned outside the cave again, putting her more on edge.

She knew he hadn't abandoned her. She trusted him about that. But he could have fallen, been injured, attacked by a savage wolf…

Worried, she pawed through the basket, then pulled on a sweater and socks. She gulped down a handful of dried figs to quell her hunger, took a swallow of water and rose.

Grabbing her flashlight, she squeezed past the rocks at the entrance, then shoved through the barrier of shrubs. She staggered free from the prickly branches, then paused to see where she was.

The nearly full moon had risen in the inky sky, and its silver light dusted the woods. Boulders and deadwood filled the spaces between the pine trees. A cold wind ruffled her hair. Not far away the river rushed past, the smell of moisture thick in the air.

Moving as quietly as she could, she threaded her way through the trees, staying parallel to the stream. An owl hooted overhead. Insects sang in the night. She searched the shadows, making out bushes and rocks as her eyes adjusted to the dark. But Deven was nowhere around.

Suddenly, the scent of wood smoke drifted past. She tensed, clicked off her flashlight, her pulse beating hard in her ears. Who was out there? Deven? Singh's men? Or someone even more ominous?

She wavered, not sure whether to investigate or return to the safety of the cave. But if Deven was in trouble, she couldn't ignore his plight.

Her pulse quickening, trying not to make noise, she padded through the woods toward the smoke. But every twig snapping underfoot, every crackling leaf, erupted like gunshots in the quiet night.

When the smoke grew stronger, she stopped, listening hard. The deep timbre of a man's voice cut the night, and she realized someone had camped ahead.

Now to find out who it was.

She scaled a fallen log, jumped over a tiny stream. When she spotted a small clearing ahead, she scooted behind a pine tree and peeked out. Two men sat on logs around a campfire—armed with guns.

She scanned the clearing, counted three yaks grazing near the men, their cargo packs piled nearby. They could be smugglers, armed rebels, human traffickers…

She glanced around, her adrenaline rushing now, but there were no captives, no sign of Deven, thank God. Relieved, she turned to creep back to the cave.

A twig crackled beside her. She whirled around—too late. Blinding pain shot through her skull, and she slumped, sucked into a twirling vortex of blackness.

And then didn't feel anything more.

Chapter 12

Deven crouched behind a boulder near the smugglers' campfire, his mind railing at the stubborn woman tied to the tree. What had she been thinking? Why had she left the cave? Why hadn't she listened to him and stayed safe?

He gritted his teeth, battling to keep a leash on his temper as he watched the three smugglers play cards by the fire. The flames glinted off the machine guns propped behind them, the empty liquor jugs they'd tossed to the side.

Thank God he'd stumbled across this encampment. If he'd headed in the other direction, if he hadn't heard the commotion when the men had captured her… He quickly quashed that chilling thought and narrowed his gaze on the men.

"I won," the skinniest of the men announced.

"Not yet. We've got two more rounds." The second man threw in his cards and lumbered to his feet. Then he staggered past the fire to the packs at the edge of the clearing and pulled out another jug. "We agreed," he reminded them, turning back. "No one touches her until then."

The others grumbled. Deven adjusted the position of his rifle, sighted down the barrel at the men. They would start shooting soon. Maya's uncommon beauty guaranteed that. He had to get her to safety before the gunfire broke out.

But she hadn't moved since he'd arrived. He spared a glance at where she lay, slumped against a tree. Her eyes were closed, her mouth slack, and even in the firelight, he could see that her cheek was caked with blood. Fury burned through him, and he sucked in a breath to control the rage. Those men would pay. He'd make damned sure of that. But first he had to get her away.

He lowered the gun and backed away from the clearing, keeping his eyes on the men. Then he crept around the campfire to the trees behind Maya and propped his rifle against a rock. His pistol in hand, he flattened himself to the ground and crawled on his belly toward where she lay.

A curse broke out from across the clearing, followed by mutters from the other men. Deven paused, his heart beating fast, keeping his head flat on the ground. When nothing else happened, he resumed inching through the stones and damp weeds.

"Maya," he whispered as he neared the tree. "Maya."

She lifted her head, then groaned.

"Shh. Quiet."

"Deven?" Her voice came out slurred, and his heart faltered. How hard had she been hit?

She turned her head, trying to see him, but her eye was swollen shut. He trembled, spurred by the need to wreak vengeance, but managed to keep his voice calm. "Don't move. I'm going to cut you loose."

He rolled to the side, tugged his knife from his pocket, then slashed the ropes binding her arms to the tree. She groaned and rubbed her wrists.

He fought down the desperate need to hold her, to pick her up and whisk her away from harm. They had to do this carefully so the men didn't see. "All right. Scoot back slowly," he murmured, aiming his gun at the men. "I'll cover for you. And don't wait for me—just hurry back to the cave."

She shifted back from the tree, then stopped. Her hand flew to her chest. "My medallion." Panic threaded her voice. "They took it. I have to get it back."

He muttered a curse. "I'll come back for it. Now go." They didn't have much time.

"Not without the medallion. What if they leave? We might never find it again."

He hissed out a breath, instinct urging him to make her flee. But they did need that medallion. It was their key to bringing down Singh. But no medallion, no matter how important, was worth endangering Maya's life. "Too risky. Let's go."

"Forget it."

"Maya—"

"Deven, be reasonable. Once they realize I'm gone it'll be too late."

He swore, wrestling with his need to protect her, knowing she was right. All hell would break loose when those men discovered that she'd escaped. The best time to find that medallion was now.

He scanned the moonlit clearing. The smuggled cargo was just beyond the circle of firelight near the grazing yaks. "All right." He hoped he wouldn't regret this. "Stay here. Don't move. Pretend you're still tied up."

"But—"

"Either wait here," he gritted out, "or I'll drag you back to that cave."

She fell silent. Hoping she'd gotten the message, he started to slide backward, then stopped. "Here." He pressed his knife into her palm, gave her hand a reassuring squeeze. Then he wormed his way back to the boulder, grabbed his rifle and melted into the woods.

He'd nearly reached the packs when he heard footsteps. He ducked behind a bush and held his breath, every sense hyperalert. The heaviest of the smugglers lurched past in the moonlight, staggering toward the privacy of the trees.

Perfect. Deven waited a heartbeat, then crept up behind the drunk man. In one swift motion, he jerked him back, covering his mouth so he couldn't yell, and rammed the butt of his gun down hard on his head. The man slumped against him, and Deven lowered him to the ground.

He turned him over and checked his pockets, then confiscated his gun. No sign of the medallion yet.

Deven waited, his breath sawing, but no one raised the alarm. He slipped through the moonlight toward the grazing yaks, then crouched behind a tree to watch.

"He'd better hurry up," the skinny smuggler mumbled. "I want to finish this game."

The other man made a sound of disgust. "Forget him. Just deal the cards. I've waited for that woman long enough."

The men turned, craning their necks to look at Maya, and Deven tensed. But she still had her head bent forward, her arms behind her. The men grunted and returned to their cards.

Deven crept closer to the shuffling yaks, eyed the bulging packs at the edge of the light. He knew it was risky. If the smugglers looked his way, they'd spot him for sure. Staying low, he darted across the clearing to the packs, then dove to the muddy ground. The men still stared at their cards.

A gust of wind crackled the campfire. The yaks snorted

and stomped their hooves. Deven crawled to the nearest pack and rifled through a cache of illegal tiger pelts. The next pack contained the same.

"Where is he?" the thin smuggler muttered. "Hey, Raj, you get lost out there?"

The other man snickered, and Deven flattened himself to the ground. The grazing yaks huffed. The smell of damp earth and wool filled his lungs.

Aware that he only had seconds, Deven reached for the remaining pack. He searched through some clothes, then his hand closed around something round, something metallic. His pulse quickening, he pulled it out. Maya's medallion—thank God.

But then a crashing noise came from the woods. Deven plastered himself to the ground and swore.

His luck had just run out.

"What was that?" the thin man asked.

"What?"

"That noise. In the woods. Hey, Raj. Is that you?" He picked up his gun, got to his feet.

Deven eyed the distance to the trees. He'd never make it. The minute he moved, they would spot him and shoot.

But then Maya stirred. "Water," she moaned.

Deven froze. What was she doing? Why was she drawing attention to herself?

The smuggler ignored her, started in Deven's direction.

"Water…please," she called again.

The thin man swiveled to face her. "Shut up."

Deven closed his eyes, disgust warring with fear. She was trying to distract the smugglers so he could get away. But didn't she realize the danger that would put her in?

Of course she did. She was the Leopard. She knew exactly what these men would do.

Respect penetrated the ice in his gut. She was gutsy, he'd give her that much—the most courageous woman he knew.

And he'd kill those men before he'd let them touch her again.

Maya whimpered, louder this time. "Thirsty…please…help me."

"Check the woods for Raj," the thin man ordered his comrade. "I'm going to shut that woman up."

While the second man lumbered to his feet, Deven crawled away from the packs. Then he raced through the woods, reaching the boulder behind Maya just as the scrawny man got to her side.

The smuggler threw back his fist to strike her. Deven exploded with rage. He lunged out from the trees, slammed into the smaller man. They crashed to the ground and rolled.

Deven erupted in a frenzy of action. He pounded the man's skull, his face, blazing with fury, fighting with a violence he could barely contain. The man was drunk, his reflexes slowed, and he couldn't match Deven's weight. But he still got off a blow to Deven's gut.

Deven grunted, ignored the flash of pain. They twisted, grappling for supremacy, and thrashed through the dirt and weeds.

A shot rang out. A bullet plowed the dirt near their heads. "Get out," Deven shouted to Maya.

"The medallion—"

"I've got it. Go!"

They rolled again. The smuggler somehow produced a gun. Deven grabbed his wrist, slammed it against the ground, straining to knock the gun free. But the man grunted, heaved up with surprising strength, tossing Deven aside. Another shot barked out nearby.

Shaking the stinging sweat from his eyes, Deven launched himself at the smuggler again, and wrested the weapon away. Then he reared up, determined to put an end to this, and kneed the man in the groin.

The man bellowed, doubled over. Deven grabbed the gun, spun around, and fired at the two men hiding near the yaks.

Then he rushed over to Maya. She knelt by the rock where he'd left the rifle, wielding his knife in her hand. Furious that she hadn't listened to him and escaped, he yanked her to her feet. "Come on."

He snatched up his gun and pulled her into the woods. But something was wrong. She stumbled, lurched off balance again, her movements unnaturally slow. Another shot came from behind.

Deven dropped her arm and raised the rifle, riddling the woods with a blast. Hoping that kept them down for a while, he turned back and caught Maya's waist. "Hold on to me."

Half carrying, half dragging her with him, he hauled her through the woods. But she still moved too slowly, whimpering and groaning with pain. When she nearly fell again, he scooped her into his arms.

Ignoring her feeble protests, he loped along the bank of the river, the bright moon lighting his path. Then he angled his way through the trees, avoiding bushes and deadfall, and plowed through an icy stream. They neared the cave, and he swung back and scanned the woods. No sign of the smugglers yet.

"Get inside." He lowered her to her feet, watched as she pushed through the bushes hiding the cave. Once she'd disappeared, he lowered himself behind a boulder to wait. The river gurgled and splashed in the distance. The wind thrashed the pines overhead. He stayed crouched in the moonlight, listening for signs of pursuit. Only when he was sure the men hadn't followed did he rise and enter the cave.

Maya huddled on the blanket, the faint glow from a candle illuminating her battered face. She looked up as he came in, and his grip on his temper slipped.

"Damn it," he raged. "Why didn't you stay here like I told you? What were you doing out there?"

She winced and clutched her forehead. "I was looking for you."

"Me?" He stared at her in disbelief. "I told you I'd be back."

"I know, but I thought you'd... I thought..."

The realization hit him like a slap. "You thought I'd left you."

"No." She kept her hand on her head. "I thought you'd been hurt. I wanted to make sure you were all right."

"So you went out there and risked your life." He worked his jaw, struggling to regain control. Of course she would worry. She spent her life rescuing people in need. But another few minutes with those men...

He blocked out the terrible thought and tried to sound calm. She didn't need a lecture right now. She was injured, in no shape to argue with him.

But damn, that had been so close....

A twig cracked outside the cave. Tensing, he motioned toward the candle. Maya leaned over and blew it out.

Darkness engulfed them. Deven moved to the entrance, keeping his steps quiet, and stared past the bushes into the night. A rustle came from behind him, and Maya stopped at his side.

He forced himself to ignore her nearness, to focus on the threat outside the cave. Because he definitely didn't want to examine the emotions swirling inside him—or remember how vulnerable she'd looked tied to that tree.

"Is anyone there?" she whispered.

He listened for another minute, then shook his head. "No. It was probably an animal." Still wrestling with his emotions, he flicked on his flashlight again. The amber beam cast a glow over her face.

"Do you think those men saw where we went?" she asked.

"No." But they would search at dawn. With a prize as lovely as Maya, no way would they give up.

Which meant he had to get her away from here fast.

"How's your head?"

"It hurts."

"I'll bet." He nodded toward the blanket. "Sit down and I'll take a look."

While she staggered to the blanket, he shoved his pistol into his waistband and lowered himself to one knee. Her scalp wound oozed with blood. The bruise on her cheek had swelled, nearly closing one eye.

"We'd better clean that up." His voice came out gruff.

"All right." She didn't move.

He handed her the flashlight, then rifled through the basket for something to use. He dampened a clean cloth with water, began to dab off the blood. She flinched, and he gentled his touch even more.

"Hold on." He wiped the bruise around her eye, trying not to cause her more pain. Then he set down the cloth and frowned. "That's all I can do for now." And it wasn't nearly enough. She needed painkillers, ice for the swelling, possibly stitches on her scalp. She probably had a concussion, too.

"We'd better go," she said, slurring her words.

He ignored that. She wasn't budging from this cave for hours. "Let's see the map."

She pulled the flattened scroll from her pocket, handed it over without a protest, then lay down and closed her eyes. Knowing she had to be in tremendous pain to ignore the map, he unrolled it and studied the marks.

"What does it say?" She kept her eyes shut.

"We're supposed to head upriver until it forks, then climb the hill to the north."

"Sounds easy."

"Sure, as long as the landscape hasn't changed in a thousand years." He rolled up the useless map in disgust.

"Deven?"

"Yeah?" He grabbed the other blanket and tucked it around her shoulders. And despite the bruise distorting her face, despite the misery in her eyes, her beauty tugged at his gut.

"The medallion…"

"I've got it." He pulled it from his pocket and held it out.

"No…you keep it…need to go—"

"Later. Rest for a while."

"No…you go." Her good eye pleaded with his. "You have to go on without me."

He sat back on his heels, too stunned to answer. She'd just entrusted him with her medallion, her most prized possession, the one thing she never removed. She believed that he'd do the right thing—despite the past, despite his warnings that he wasn't worthy.

Warmth twined around his heart.

Humbled, disgusted with himself for wanting this woman he couldn't have, he reluctantly released her hand. "Forget it." He wasn't letting her out of his sight.

She clutched his arm. Her grip was weak, her fingers

cold. "There's no time. You have to stop Singh. And the eclipse—"

"We've got plenty of time," he lied. "Don't worry about it. Now close your eyes and rest."

He took the medallion, worked the chain carefully over her head, then slid it beneath her tunic, where it belonged. His fingers lingered on her throat, and he felt the delicate beat of her pulse.

"Thank you," she whispered. She squeezed his hand. Her skin was too chilled, her hand fragile and small. His throat suddenly thick, he leaned over, pulled the blanket closer around her neck.

Her breathing deepened, slowed, and she drifted off to sleep. And for a long moment he just gazed at her, his own breathing ragged, his emotions skidding out of control.

He'd messed up completely. He should have realized she wouldn't stay put. Now, come morning, the smugglers would hunt for their tracks. And Maya could never outrun them. She could hardly stand on her feet.

Even worse, the sound of that gunfire would have carried, tipping off Singh's men—erasing any advantage they'd had. The helicopters would pursue them at dawn.

And if all that weren't bad enough, they were running out of time. The lunar eclipse was the following night. They had an outdated map to guide them. They'd need a miracle to find that sadhu's cave.

And heaven only knew what danger awaited them if they did.

But as he watched Maya's face slacken in sleep and listened to her soft breath, an even worse worry consumed him.

Assuming they survived this ordeal, how would he ever let this woman go?

Chapter 13

Maya prided herself on her strength. In the orphanages she'd lived in growing up, she'd always been the strong one, the fighter who protected the weaker girls. And she'd stayed staunchly self-sufficient ever since, refusing to rely on anyone else.

She'd been humbled now.

Pain shot through her scalp as she limped up the mountain. Her depleted muscles quivered and ached. Her bruised eye stung; her forehead throbbed like a lava dome ready to blow. And she had to admit that without Deven's help, she'd never make it up the hill.

She straggled to a stop, waited for him to cross a gurgling creek. The stream wasn't big—maybe a foot or two deep, ten feet across—but still too far to jump. Not that she intended to leap anywhere with her skull threatening to explode.

He strode easily from rock to rock, then hopped the final

distance to the opposite bank. "Be careful," he warned. "The rocks are slippery."

"All right."

She inhaled the scent of cold moisture, started across the flat rocks—but with her eye swollen shut, her depth perception was off. She tottered, slipped. Deven lunged back and grabbed her hand, then pulled her safely ashore.

"Thanks."

He didn't release her, and his big, warm hand enveloped hers. She tipped her head back, and his dark gaze skimmed over her face. "How are you holding up?" he asked, and his husky voice rumbled through her nerves.

"Fine."

He raised a brow, but didn't argue. "We'll stop at the rise ahead."

He let go of her hand and continued hiking, and she trudged behind him up the hill. She tried to ignore the fierce pain cleaving her skull, the inconvenient guilt that wouldn't subside.

But she couldn't deny the truth. Her independent nature had cost them. She'd refused to stay in the cave, hadn't listened to Deven. As a result, she'd been captured, injured. She'd nearly lost the priceless medallion.

Even worse, she'd put Deven at risk. Those smugglers could have killed him. Her stomach pitched on a swell of remorse.

And the repercussions of her stubbornness hadn't ended. Even now she was slowing them down. Without her, Deven could have hiked faster, located that hermit's cave hours ago. Instead, they'd spent the entire day inching up the mountain— and the cave was nowhere in sight.

Even worse, the map had proved useless. Forests had filled in clearings. Boulders and streams had disappeared. Even the river had changed course over the centuries, causing them to make false turns and backtrack as they hunted for landmarks that weren't there.

They reached the crest of a hill, and Deven stopped. "We'll rest here for a minute."

"I can keep going."

He didn't respond to that obvious lie. He merely handed her the bottle of water, and she drank deeply, greedily, chugging the cold liquid down her parched throat. Then she handed it back, staggered to a nearby rock and collapsed.

Deven stood near her, scanning the mountain. He drank some water, recapped the bottle, and a stray drop coursed down his cheek. His beard stubble had grown over the past few days, making his face darker, even sexier—which wasn't fair. He turned more rugged as the days wore on, while she looked as if she'd crawled from a swamp. She would sell her soul for a bath.

She sighed and pushed the loose strands of hair from her sweaty face. Her appearance didn't matter. They had far more serious problems—such as getting to that cave before the eclipse. Deven should have taken her medallion and left her. She understood his desire to protect her, but they were running out of time.

"I think I see the cave," he said suddenly.

"Really?" She pushed herself to her feet, hobbled to where he stood. "Where is it?"

"See that crooked tree?" He motioned toward the slope ahead. "It's just above it, to the left, in the ten o'clock position."

He leaned closer, pointed to a spot beyond the tree. And despite the terrible pain racking her skull, despite the fatigue dragging the blood through her veins, his nearness sparked a flurry of nerves. She eyed the masculine slant of his cheekbones, the dark lashes fringing his hypnotic eyes, that wickedly carnal mouth.

His gaze clashed with hers. Her heart made a frenzied kick.

And a kaleidoscope of memories slammed through her— his warm, male skin, the seductive silk of his hair. The feel of his strong arms cradling her as he carried her back to the cave.

Breathless, knowing she couldn't go there, she tore her gaze away. She squinted into the late-afternoon sunshine and spotted the distant cave. "You think that's it?"

"If it isn't, we're out of luck. It's going to be dark soon."

She eyed the sky. He was right. The sun was already dipping toward the peaks. "We'd better hurry, then."

Grunting his agreement, he started toward the slope. She followed more slowly, trying to maintain her balance in the rough terrain. Rocks skidded loose beneath her sandals. She slid on a patch of damp weeds. The slope turned vertical, and she had to grab at branches and pockets of brush to keep from tumbling down.

By the time they made it to the cave, she could hardly stand upright. Her thigh muscles twitched. Her lungs burned as if she'd swallowed fire. She studied the small cave set into the mountain, knowing that if someone dangerous lurked inside, she didn't have the strength to escape.

Deven set down their basket and tugged out his pistol, the rifle still strapped to his back. "Stay back while I check inside." But just as he moved toward the opening, a sadhu hermit stepped out.

The holy man stopped, looking startled. Although she'd seen sadhus before, Maya struggled not to gasp back.

The mystic was tall, cadaverously thin, dressed only in a loincloth. Ashes covered his leathered skin. Gray dreadlocks flowed past his knees. He had a bushy mustache and beard, another pile of dreadlocks knotted on the side of his head, like a coiled rope about to slip off.

He'd painted a bright red mark on his forehead—a spiritual bull's-eye surrounded by white. Orange paint ringed his bloodshot eyes, and the rest of his face was bright white.

"Namaste," she said, pressing her palms together in greeting. The hermit nodded and greeted her back.

Uncertain how to begin, she tugged the scroll from her pocket and held it out. "The abbot from the monastery sent us here. He gave us this map. He said you'd tell us about my medallion." Careful not to bump her injured eye, she slid the medallion from her neck.

If the hermit was surprised, he didn't show it. He took the map and medallion, then motioned for them to sit. Maya sank onto one of the flat rocks outside the cave, and Deven positioned himself close by.

The hermit lowered himself to the ground, tucking his legs into the lotus position. While he studied the silver medallion, Maya glanced at the sheer mountains towering around them, the snow glinting in the high ravines.

"You spoke to the abbot?" the hermit asked.

"Yes." She hesitated, not sure how much to reveal. "We needed to decipher the inscription on my medallion. We thought he might know something about the language. But by the time we got to the monastery, armed men had taken it over. They injured the abbot in the attack. Badly. I don't think... He might not survive."

Thanks to her drawing. Flashing back to the murdered bookseller, she suffered another spurt of guilt.

The hermit didn't speak for several moments. A hawk wheeled past in the sky. He turned the medallion over again and looked up. "What did the abbot tell you?"

"Not much," she admitted. "Just that it came from the eleventh century, but the cult that made it was destroyed. The monks passed down the knowledge about the medallion, though, and the map. He said you would tell us the rest. And that we had to hurry, get here before the lunar eclipse tonight."

The hermit nodded, as if satisfied with her response. "You've heard the legend about the Roma treasures?"

Her pulse raced. Deven leaned forward, his eyes intent. "So this has to do with the crown?"

"Yes." The hermit's gaze shifted back to hers. "Those were times of great political turmoil. The king had enemies, even within his own camp. Some thought he was too impulsive, not worthy to lead. There were plots to steal the treasures and overthrow him. And there was that curse….

"Then the Muslims came. The Roma army couldn't hold them off, and the king realized they faced defeat. He gave the necklace and dagger to his most trusted advisers. He left the crown here at the temple of Parvati with the Hindu monks.

"But he had a premonition that he wouldn't return, that he wouldn't survive the war. He needed something to pass on to his successor, some token the next king could use to prove he was the rightful owner of the sacred crown."

"So they made the medallion," Deven said.

"Yes. The monks hid the crown in a secret vault in the Parvati temple. To locate the vault, you need this medallion. To open it, you need the key."

"The key?" They had something else to hunt for? They'd never find it in time!

The hermit nodded, his dreadlocks brushing the ground. "The king didn't return, of course. The Roma were driven out of Romanistan and scattered across the world. But the monks preserved the knowledge of the crown's location, passing it from head monk to head monk, even after the cult was destroyed. And a sadhu has always stayed here at the cave to guard the key."

Maya's hopes took off. "You have it here?"

"Wait." He handed her the medallion, rose in a fluid motion and padded back into his cave.

She slipped the medallion over her neck. "What do you think?"

Deven shrugged. "I guess it makes sense, given the times. They'd need something to use as a safeguard."

And it had worked. The crown had stayed hidden for a thousand years.

Seconds later, the hermit returned. He lowered himself to the ground again, then held out a small bundle made of bleached goat hide. Her curiosity building, Maya took the package from his outstretched hands. Hindu symbols had been painted on the satiny hide—the lotus, Shiva's trident, the sacred mark for Om. A gold cord tied it shut.

Her heart beat fast. She glanced at Deven, saw the same anticipation gleaming in his eyes. She untied the cord, carefully unrolled the hide. Inside was an iron key.

It was longer than her hand, heavier than she would have imagined. It had an odd slit along the shank and a large round handle engraved with more ancient symbols—the sun, the crescent moon. The key gleamed in the waning sunlight, as bright and shiny as if it had just been forged.

"Listen carefully," the hermit instructed. "Take the medallion and the key into the temple. There you'll find the lunar dial. Use the medallion to align the dial, then wait for the eclipse. Right before the moon turns black, the dial will cast a shadow pointing to the vault."

Maya hesitated, suddenly uneasy. "I don't know.… Maybe we shouldn't do this. I mean, it's not really our crown. Maybe we should take this to the Roma princess, let her decide what to do."

The hermit stood. "Fate has brought you here for a reason. You have the medallion, the map and the key. Now you must find the crown. But work quickly. An aura of danger surrounds you."

A gust of wind moaned in the trees. She shivered at the unnerving sound and rubbed her arms. But the hermit was right. They couldn't let Singh get the crown.

"Has anyone else been here?" Deven asked as if reading her mind.

The hermit shook his head. "No. No one has passed this way in years. Enter through the cave," he added. He motioned behind him, then pressed his palms together in farewell. "My mission is done. You must do the rest." He turned and strode down the slope.

He was leaving? Maya sprang up to stop him. "Wait! What about the inscription on the medallion? You didn't tell us what it says."

The hermit paused on the slope below her and glanced back. "It says, 'Both darkness and light provide insight into the heart.'" He lifted his hand in farewell, then disappeared from view.

Maya didn't move. What darkness? Whose heart? What in the world did he mean?

The wind gusted again, and a low wail escaped from the cave—like a shriek of doom. And a sudden wave of trepidation went through her, a feeling of dread.

Shaken, she turned to face Deven again. His eyes burned dark with determination. Tension poured off his rigid frame.

So he felt the danger, too.

But there was no turning back. They were committed, in this together.

No matter what perils lurked ahead.

As soon as the hermit left, Deven strode into the cave and flicked on his flashlight, unable to shake a nagging sense of danger. He wished he knew the terrain, wished to hell he knew what lay ahead. How could he protect Maya when he was charging in blind?

Scowling, he aimed the light around the cave, illuminating the murals painted on the walls—scenes from the Hindu epics, avatars of the gods. Krishna, Vishnu, Parvati, her son Ganesh with his elephant head.

"This is amazing," Maya marveled from beside him. "It must have taken decades to create all this."

Deven grunted, more interested in finding that temple than studying the art. He angled the beam toward the back of the cave and spotted a short, low tunnel chiseled from the rocks. A faint patch of daylight shone from the other end.

"Through here." He doubled over, then started through the passage, but that insistent feeling of menace still buffeted his nerves. The ceiling dipped lower, and his rifle clinked against the rocks.

Several yards later, the tunnel ended. He straightened, helped Maya out and glanced around. They were in a long, narrow slot canyon, about ten feet wide, with sheer, towering cliffs soaring about them on either side. Cobblestones paved the ground. Symbols had been carved into the cliffs at regular intervals, like signposts guiding the way.

"It's a road," he said, stunned at the discovery.

Still marveling, he led the way down the narrow canyon, the soft thud of their footsteps breaking the oppressive quiet. Along the way he spotted more signs of human activity—ancient writing on the rocks, water channels chiseled into the walls. When they came to a stone archway spanning the road, they both stopped.

"A gate," Maya said, sounding as dumbfounded as he felt. "It's the entrance to a hidden city."

"Incredible." Hindu statues formed the base of the gateway. Precisely engineered stones arched overhead. The air was still, throbbing with a deep sense of expectation. He turned around, trying to spot another way into the city, but high cliffs hemmed them in.

They passed under the gate without speaking, and the road became a city street. Dozens of caves pockmarked the cliffs in either direction like ancient apartments. Stone pillars fronted some of the openings, forming elaborate facades. They trekked without speaking through the deserted city, passing cave after yawning cave. The eerie silence swallowed their steps.

"How are we going to know where the temple is?" Maya whispered.

"I don't know." He scanned the cliffs, searching for something to guide them. The caves' black gullets gaped back.

Then the sound of trickling water drew his attention. Following the noise, he spotted a pile of scattered rocks to the side—the remnants of a wall. He shifted his gaze to where the wall continued, saw the now-dry fountain underneath. Some long-forgotten mason had built an aqueduct, providing water to this secluded place.

And that bothered him. As well engineered as this city was, there had to be another way in.

Or more importantly, another way out.

Frowning, he continued plodding along, futilely searching for trails. Time had left the city untouched for centuries, completely hidden from the outside world. It was an ancient wonder. A tense, mystical feeling pulsed in the air.

Moments later, they reached the end of the canyon. Directly ahead of them, a stone stairway went up the cliff. Symbols had been carved into the base of the steps—the crescent moon, the sun, more exotic writing. The steps spiraled dozens of feet above them and then twisted out of sight.

"This must be it," Maya said, her voice low.

"Yeah." He turned her way. Her face was flushed, her hair half loose. And a feeling of tenderness stole through his heart. "You want to wait here while I check it out?"

"Not a chance."

He understood. In her place, he'd also feel the need to see this through. "You go first, then." That way if she stumbled, he'd block her fall.

"All right."

She started up the staircase, and he followed, staying close on her heels. There wasn't a handrail to hold on to. The steps were shallow and close together, designed for smaller feet. To make things even more treacherous, the steps dipped in the center, as if thousands of people had made this pilgrimage before them, wearing down the stones.

Maya paused on the step above him. "You all right?" he asked.

"Just…catching my breath." She waited a beat, then started climbing again.

The staircase continued upward, stretching several stories above the ground. It made a sharp turn near the top of the canyon, then ended at a wide ledge in front of another cave.

Devon studied the sheer mountains ringing the canyon, the open sky above. The ledge looked like a place of worship—even sacrifice.

He thrust that thought aside.

Maya crossed the ledge and entered the temple. He followed, then came to a stop inside. The cave was shaped like an observatory—circular, about thirty feet in diameter, the walls covered with symbols and astrological signs. A long slit sliced the domed ceiling, exposing a glimpse of the sky. In the center of the room sat a raised platform with a huge stone dial.

Maya rubbed her arms. "Do you feel that…tension in the air?"

"Yeah." The room vibrated with that same sense of anticipation he'd felt when they'd entered the city's gate—only stronger, more insistent.

Uneasy, he strode to the platform and climbed the steps. The dial consisted of two stone rings, one inside the other, the largest several feet wide. In the center there was a round, empty spot the size of Maya's medallion. A bronze fin stuck out from the side.

Maya joined him on the platform and studied the rings. "They have the same symbols as my medallion."

She was right. "Except they're in a different order."

"The sadhu said we had to line them up to match."

Deven tugged the outer ring to turn it, but it didn't move. He pulled again, getting his weight behind it, but it still refused to budge.

He bent down and examined the center spot. "There's some sort of locking mechanism in it. Put your medallion in there, and let's see what it does."

Maya tugged off her medallion and removed the chain. Then she set it in the center of the dial, rotating it until it dropped into place. Deven grabbed the outer ring again and pulled.

The stones creaked, started to turn. He kept up the pressure, shifting it until the symbols aligned with the medallion, then stopped.

He wiped his forehead on his sleeve, impressed. "Simple, but effective." Without the medallion, the dial wouldn't turn, preventing someone from trying random combinations.

He eyed the hole in the ceiling above. "It must work like a sundial. The moonlight shines through that hole and strikes the dial."

"And then this metal piece casts a shadow on the vault."

"Right." Deven leaped off the platform, strode around the cave and studied the walls. But he couldn't see any cracks or indentations, nothing that would indicate a vault. "If it's here, they hid it well."

Restless now, he strode to the ledge outside the temple and looked at the city below. Dusk lengthened the shadows in the canyon. The sheer rock walls boxed them in. There was no other trail out of the city, no way down from the temple except by those stairs.

And that bugged the hell out of him. Medieval people had enemies. They would never build a city without an escape route. And if there was another way out… What if Singh had found it? What if he'd beaten them here?

The shadows deepened. The sun dipped close to the mountains, lingered a final second, then disappeared. And an ominous feeling swirled in his gut, as if with the light went their final hope.

Maya came up beside him. "What do we do now?"

"Wait for the eclipse."

And hope that Singh hadn't trapped them. Because if he had…Devon would be forced to confront him.

And Maya would finally learn the terrible truth he'd spent the last twelve years trying to hide.

Chapter 14

Maya huddled on the ledge outside the temple, staring out at the deepening night. Thousands of stars glittered in the velvet blackness. The full moon loomed above them—huge, luminous—its shadowy eyes stark, its mouth stalled in a desperate scream.

She hugged her knees, shivering in the chilly air. The ache in her head had dulled, but now emotions chugged through her belly—excitement, anticipation, fear. She could hardly believe that in a few short minutes they might find the fabled crown.

Or Singh might appear.

She knew Deven expected trouble. He'd been checking his weapons, pacing across the ledge, scrutinizing the terrain. Anxiety vibrated right out of him and charged the air.

The rumble of unseen helicopters didn't help.

He strode past her again, and she turned her head to watch. Moonlight glimmered off his midnight hair and dusted the noble line of his nose. And despite the fear, despite the uncertainty of the coming night, she knew one thing—she loved him. She always had. He was everything she'd ever dreamed of in a man; he was smart, courageous, strong. Just one look from his eyes changed the speed of her heartbeat. His nearness ignited her nerves. They'd been good friends, trusted comrades, explosive lovers. She'd never even been tempted by another man.

But he'd been honest with her. He'd made it clear from the start of this journey that he couldn't have a future with her. And once they found that crown, he would go.

Which meant their time together was nearly up.

A dull ache deadened her chest, the painful pull of longing she'd been trying to suppress. She'd deceived herself, told herself that she wouldn't mind when he left.

She'd been wrong. She now knew that she would never get over this man.

She hitched out her breath, returned her gaze to the moon. She would survive, of course. She would pick up the pieces and go on, just as she'd done every time life had dealt her a blow.

But she would miss him. And a part of her would never be the same.

Just then, a shadow crept over the edge of the moon, blurring the border. "The eclipse is starting," Deven's deep voice rasped in the dark.

"I see it." She rose, her heart accelerating, her stomach a bundle of nerves. The ancient key lay heavy in her pocket. The medallion rested against her chest. She entered the temple behind Deven, her footsteps thudding on the dirt.

Silver moonlight flooded the cave through the slit in the ceiling. She walked to the platform, glanced up through the opening at the shrieking moon. The darkness continued across its face, stirring the hair on her nape.

Deven climbed up on the platform, then reached down and tugged her up. Her pulse in overdrive now, she pulled the medallion from around her neck and placed it in the center of the dial. Deven turned the massive stone rings, making minor adjustments until the astrological symbols aligned.

"Now what?" she asked.

"Now we watch."

Her mouth dry, her palms clammy, she scanned the hundreds of mathematical equations and symbols painted on the moonlit walls. What if the dial didn't work? What if they'd positioned it wrong? What if this was a hoax, some sort of medieval practical joke?

Her gaze gravitated to the moon again. The black shadow kept advancing, gnawing at its face. And she knew deep down that this wasn't a joke. There was something otherworldly about this eclipse, something powerful. She could see why people once believed it was a portent of evil, a message of doom from the gods.

Suddenly, a vision formed in the temple's shadows—a flickering bonfire. Priests in white robes chanting. The beating of primitive drums. Ancient people huddling in terror, making sacrifices to the gods...

The vision vanished. Her body trembled. The hair on her nape rose on end. "Did you see that?" she whispered to Deven, shuddering. Even now she felt something filling the room, a presence—like the souls of people long gone.

"I saw it." His eyes were fierce, his body rippling with tension, like a primitive warrior preparing to fight.

The room dimmed as the moon darkened. Quivering harder now, she shifted her gaze to the sky. The shadow had crawled relentlessly forward, devouring the moon. Excitement mingled with dread in her blood.

And then only the barest sliver was left.

"The crescent moon." She frowned at a niggling memory, but then the dial cast a shadow, a black line slicing the cave.

"There it is." Deven leaped off the platform and raced along the line to the wall.

But the moon went completely black, thrusting the cave into total darkness. And then just as abruptly, it came back. It was full again, but tinged a deep bloodred.

Maya's heart stopped. She'd never seen anything like it. Fierce dread battered her throat.

"Come on. Help me look," Deven called, and she dragged her gaze away. He flicked on his flashlight, shined the beam at the stones where the shadow had been, and she hurried to join him at the wall. She ran her hands along the cool, bumpy surface, tracing painted symbols, feeling for soft spots or cracks.

Nothing.

She knelt, continued searching the wall near the ground, losing hope as the minutes passed. But the vault *had* to be here. They couldn't have come all this way and leave without the crown.

"Maybe it's buried," she said.

"I'll dig." Using the handle of the flashlight as a shovel, Deven scratched the hard-packed dirt at the base of the rock. She unwrapped the ancient key from the goat hide, then used the rounded end to help him loosen the soil.

They'd dug several inches down when a clink rang out.

A thrill ran through her. "There's something here. Something metallic." She couldn't keep the excitement from her voice.

"Give me some space."

She shifted away, and Deven dug faster, breaking up the tightly packed soil. Minutes later, he'd uncovered a metal plate in the ground, about two feet square. He brushed aside the dirt, aimed the flashlight at it, and a keyhole emerged.

Her excitement at a fever pitch, she helped whisk away more soil. Their eyes met, held. Anticipation crackled the air. "Go ahead," he said.

Her hands trembling, she inserted the key in the lock but couldn't get it to turn. Nothing happened. She jiggled it and tried again. "It doesn't work."

"Let me try. It's probably clogged with dirt." He handed her the flashlight and grasped the key. Then he twisted it, worked it back and forth in the lock, took it out and tried again. The key clicked and he pulled up the lid. The tension unbearable, she shone the light inside.

Inside the vault was a large silk bundle. Maya propped the flashlight on the ground, reached in with shaking hands and lifted it out. It was heavier than she'd expected. Her heart pounded so hard she couldn't breathe.

She set it on the ground beside the flashlight. The crimson silk was embroidered with gold and silver threads, studded with pearls and precious stones. "I've seen this type of fabric in museums," she said. "It's called *zardozi*." It had been used in ancient times to decorate all things royal—clothes, scabbards, tents, even the trappings worn by royal elephants.

Careful not to damage the fragile fabric, she untied the golden cord and carefully peeled back the silk.

The crown.

Her lungs stalled. A dull roar filled her skull. "Oh, my," she breathed. It was gorgeous, glorious, a solid gold diadem, ornately tooled, inlaid with amber of every hue—yellow, green, black.

Her gaze flew to Deven's, and she saw the same stunned exhilaration in his eyes. "Pick it up," he urged.

Almost afraid to touch it, she lifted it from its pillow, marveling at the incredible workmanship, the intricacy of the designs. The sun and moon danced along the edges. Across the center were scenes from the goddess Parvati's life. Over a dozen golden bells hung from the bottom—charms to ward off hostile spirits. The center pendant held a deep red gem.

The crown was spectacular, ancient. She could feel the unearthly power in it vibrating her hands.

She set it gingerly onto the pillow and simply stared at it, still too dazzled to move.

The fabled crown—the most sacred of the three lost treasures. The Roma people would be thrilled.

She understood instantly what it would mean to them—pride in their heritage, hope for their future. The chance to regain their dignity and respect from the outside world.

Without warning, the cave went black. Only the beam from the flashlight cut through the darkness. She glanced up at the slit in the ceiling, realizing the eclipse had continued. The moon had darkened again.

And then, in the distance, a wolf howled. The long, desolate cry filled the cave, standing her hair on end. She gripped Deven's arm, consumed with a sense of something supernatural.

"Let's get out of here," he said.

"Yes." Agitated, feeling an urgency she couldn't ignore, she bundled the crown in the embroidered silk cloth and rose.

But partway to the door, she stopped. "The medallion." She handed Deven the crown, darted back to the platform and leaped back up. She lifted the medallion from the dial, then hurried after Deven from the cave.

While he grabbed the basket and set the crown inside,

she glanced up at the sky—and froze. The moon was silver again, a glimmering crescent in the inky sky. But now meteors streaked around it, trailing ribbons of blue, pink, red. Smokelike dust shimmered behind.

She looked at it in awe. She'd never seen or heard of anything like it. And suddenly, the legend popped into her mind again. *The prophecy.*

"Deven." She couldn't tear her gaze from the sky. "The legend. Do you remember the ending?" She thought back, began to recite:

"When the full moon bleeds and the lonely dog cries
And the stars trail dust in the night
A leader will rise from the scattered hordes
And the People will regain their might."

She stopped. The meteors shot through the sky, showering them with a brilliant display of light. She stood thunderstruck, unable to process it all. The crescent moon began to grow.

The crescent moon…

Her heart stumbled hard. An acute feeling of danger swamped her again. "Deven…we need to go. I keep thinking, remembering the abbot's words…what he said about the danger, that treachery abounds."

"What?" Deven's head jerked up. "What did you just say?"

"The abbot, when he called me back. He warned me about the danger."

Deven stood stock-still, his body tense, his eyes locked on hers. "He used those words? Those exact words? That treachery abounds?"

The shock in his voice made her stomach clench. "Yes. He

said, 'Watch for the crescent moon. Treachery abounds.' But what—"

"That's my code phrase, the one I use with Skinner, my Magnum boss."

"Your boss?" Thrown off balance, she frowned. "But how could the abbot know that? Unless your boss…"

She pressed her hand to her lips. Had Deven's boss attacked the abbot?

Deven hissed, shoved his hand through his hair. "How could I have missed it? It all makes sense now. The helicopters— *that's* how Singh got them, from *us*. And that wild-goose chase of information. No wonder I couldn't find out anything."

"But…" She shook her head, still not understanding. "What are you saying? That your boss is after the crown?"

"He must be. And he must be working with Singh." Disgust tinged his voice. "They set me up."

"So you figured it out." A man stepped from the shadows near the wall. The moonlight glinted off the gun aimed directly at her head.

Her heart froze. *Sanjeet Singh.*

She'd never actually met the man—only seen him at a distance—but she couldn't mistake him now. He was muscular and tall, had an arrestingly handsome face and thick black hair spiked with gray. He wore casual slacks, an ordinary shirt—but there was nothing common about this man. He prowled toward her in the moonlight, moving with authority, arrogance, like a man used to wielding absolute power.

And those eyes… He stopped inches away, and the depravity in his eyes made her head light. She'd heard stories about his cruelty for years, the torture he'd inflicted on women so traumatized that they'd begged Maya to let them die.

Their eyes held. Sheer dread battered her throat. She'd never felt pure evil before, but this man had an aura of malevolence that iced her soul.

And she knew with sudden clarity that he would never let her survive this night.

"So here we are at last," he said, his cultured voice at odds with his sinister eyes. "The three of us, just as we were destined to be."

Destined? Maya fought through the haze of panic, struggling to think and make sense of Singh's words, but her instincts urged her to bolt. She eyed the distance to the steps, the black space yawning off the ledge, the deadly gun trained at her head.

She couldn't run for it. As soon as she moved, Singh would shoot. But she couldn't let this despicable man win.

"Leave her out of this," Deven said, his voice deadly. "This is between you and me—not her." He stood across the ledge from them, his weapon aimed at Singh, fury pouring off him in waves.

"You're wrong." Singh didn't take his eyes off her. "She's been involved in this from the start. You must know who she is."

When Deven didn't answer, he sighed. "I expected better from you. But you'll appreciate the irony. She's the missing Roma princess."

"Princess?" Maya let out a high-pitched laugh. "Are you crazy? I'm not related to the royal family. I've never even met them." The man was out of his mind.

"It's true," he said, not moving the gun from her head. "They've kept it a secret. But my spies have infiltrated their inner circle and learned the truth."

She gaped at him. The man was deluded as well as depraved. "That's ridiculous. The royals are in California.

I don't have any connection to them. Just because I have the medallion doesn't mean—"

"How do you think you got it? They gave you that medallion at birth. And they've been trying to find you ever since— checking orphanages, adoption records, death records. But they didn't know where you were.

"But I did," he continued, cutting off her protests. "Thanks to your role as *the Leopard*. I knew it couldn't be a coincidence that the Leopard had an antique medallion of Parvati, the same as the missing princess. And you were Roma, you were an orphan, you lived in Kintalabad—all the pieces fit."

Maya glanced at Deven's furious face, then back to Singh. "You're wrong." He'd definitely lost his mind.

"The woman in California is an imposter," Singh said. "An orphan they chose to replace you when you disappeared. Whether you believe it or not, it's true. You're the princess, the last of the Roma line. And that line dies with you tonight."

He was right. She didn't believe it. But crazy or not, Singh did. And he fully intended to kill her. Cold sweat moistened her spine.

"She has to die," Singh said to Deven. "You must know that. Only when she's gone can the prophecy be fulfilled."

"Prophecy?" Deven scoffed.

"Yes." Singh's gaze locked on Deven. Seizing the distraction, knowing this could be her only chance, Maya inched away from the cliff.

But his gaze swiveled back. "Not another step, Princess."

She froze, her pulse pounding. Deven flashed her a warning scowl. She understood. Singh was completely unstable, unpredictable. He could shoot her at any time. But she couldn't just stand here while he killed them and took that crown.

Singh's gaze swiveled to Deven again, and the lines of his face suddenly softened, turning almost fond. "You found the crown. You found the princess, even if you didn't know who she was. You did everything I'd hoped."

"What is that supposed to mean?" Deven demanded.

Singh made a clucking sound. "You don't really think you escaped me that night? I let you get away. And I've been watching you, following your progress ever since."

Maya frowned, trying to make sense of this twist, confused by the pride in Singh's voice. She understood why Deven was after Singh—he wanted revenge for his mother's death. But why did Singh care what happened to Deven? Why had he followed his progress? What was she missing here?

"We recruited you, trained you," Singh continued. "When the time was right, we brought you here."

"You set me up."

"I tested you. I needed you to prove your worth, to make sure you were worthy before I could tell you the rest."

"Worthy?" Deven's voice dripped with scorn. "Worthy of what?"

"To lead. To become the king."

"King." He sounded appalled.

Maya felt just as stunned. She'd never heard anything so bizarre. Singh had invented a fantasy, some sort of royal intrigue involving Deven and her.

"King of the Order of the Black Crescent Moon," Singh said. He ripped open his shirt, exposing the black tattoo on his chest.

The crescent moon with the sinister slash.

Her gut went sick at the sight. Did he head that vile organization, the group responsible for thousands of deaths?

"It has all happened, just as it was foretold," Singh said. "And now our people will take their rightful place and rule the world."

"Rightful place?" Maya scoffed, unable to contain her

outrage. "You're nothing but cowards, murderers, killers of innocent people." And this despicable man was the worst. He'd abused children, women, condemned them to lives of unspeakable hell. "And you'll never succeed."

"Oh, but we will. We have the crown. With its power we'll get all the treasures back—the treasures your people stole from us."

He raised his gun, aimed right between her eyes. "I'm the king, descended from pure, royal blood. But this is my final act. I'm not the king revealed in the prophecy. The royal astrologers studied the signs…"

He looked at Deven. "It's you. You are the destined leader. You've proven yourself. You found the princess, the crown. When she dies tonight, the prophecy will be complete. It's all yours, the treasures, the power."

"I don't want it."

"You don't have a choice."

The men stared at each other, fury pouring from Deven, a wild excitement coming from Singh.

Maya looked from one man to the other, unable to miss the terrible tension, still confused by why Deven mattered to Singh. She was missing something—something vital.

"Tell your lover the rest," Singh prodded. "Tell her!"

Deven slowly swiveled his head. His eyes locked on hers—and the haunting bleakness in them rocked her heart.

"I told you my mother took something Singh wanted." His voice turned raw. "It was *me*. He wanted me. I'm his son."

Chapter 15

Deven watched Maya's face fill with shock and disgust as she recoiled from his news. He'd expected her to despise him. Singh was a sick, vicious man. Of course she'd turn from him, repulsed.

And now she had an even greater reason to detest him. Singh was the king of the Order of the Black Crescent Moon, her people's hated enemy.

And he was that enemy's son.

Hardening his jaw against a wave of self-loathing, he stared at Singh, the evil man who'd sired him—the man whose blood ran through his veins. And in Singh's cold, flat eyes, Deven saw everything he despised.

Everything he feared he could be.

This was the man who'd murdered his mother, destroyed countless innocent lives. And now he planned to kill the woman Deven loved.

"Do it," Singh urged him, sounding almost gleeful. "Kill me and seize the crown. Make the prophecy come true."

Deven's pulse thundered with the need for vengeance. Cold fury slammed through his blood. This man had set him up. He'd followed him, drawn him into his network, manipulating him all these years.

And even now he was controlling him, forcing an impossible choice. If he killed Singh, if he succumbed to the hatred seething inside him, he would turn into what he most feared. He would fulfill his genetic destiny and become like Singh.

Worse, the moment Singh died, Deven would inherit his heinous kingdom by virtue of his bloodline and become king of the Order of the Black Crescent Moon.

Singh had backed him into a corner. If he killed Singh, he would become him.

And if he didn't, Maya would die.

His hand trembled on his pistol. His blood roared in his skull. The darkness pulled at him, blurring his vision, the primitive fury compelling him to act.

He drew a deep, shuddering breath, willing himself not to surrender, not to succumb to the urge. Long seconds passed. His body shook.

But he didn't yield. He wasn't his father after all.

Then the terrible irony struck him. Maybe he wasn't like Singh—but the Order had to end tonight.

Which meant he had no choice.

Singh had to die at his hands.

Resolve settled inside him. He allowed himself a final glance at Maya, the woman he'd always loved. She stood like a warrior in the moonlight, her dark eyes flashing, her chin raised in proud defiance. And a deep pang of longing seeped through his heart.

He didn't know if she was the princess, but he could believe it. She battled to save the downtrodden, to rescue those most abused. She was a crusader, an avenger—a true noble in every way.

Thousands of years of royal blood could very well flow in her veins.

Her eyes met his—her courageous, determined eyes. His heart splintering, he drank in the sight of the woman he yearned for, the woman he could never have.

But then she stepped closer to Singh, telegraphing her intention, knocking the breath from his lungs. She was going to save him—give him time to take down Singh—by sacrificing herself.

His gut clenched. Horror blazed through his nerves. "Maya, don't!"

But she lunged forward. Singh's gun barked. She screamed, slumped to the ground, and Deven's heart slammed to a halt.

He jerked up his gun, blinded by the need to avenge her. But before he could shoot, Singh turned and hurled himself over the ledge.

Deven gaped at the now-empty ledge in horror. Singh hit the ground with a thud.

An awful hush filled the night.

Deven stood paralyzed, staring at the space where he'd been, too shocked, too stunned to move. Singh had killed himself to fulfill the prophecy, to make Deven the dreaded king. And Maya...

He raced to her, fueled by panic. A black stain pooled the dirt where she lay. Her face looked as white as the moon.

Frantic, he knelt, checked for a pulse. She was breathing— but barely.

"Maya." He jerked off his shirt and pressed the wadded

cloth to her shoulder, desperate to stanch the bleeding. But there was so much blood.…

"Maya," he begged. "Don't die on me. Please don't die."

Her eyes opened. "Deven…" Her eyelids fluttered, and she went slack.

Dread seized him. He pulled her into his arms and leaped up, desperate to save her, knowing he had to find help for her fast. But they were alone in the canyon, miles from civilization.

A faint pulsing sound reached his ears.

The helicopter. Singh's men. They had to be close by.

And thanks to their delusion, they believed Deven was their destined leader. They would now answer to him.

He turned, hurried toward the stairs. He didn't want Singh's power, loathed everything it stood for.

But he would bargain with the devil himself to keep Maya alive.

Three days later, Deven still hovered beside Maya's hospital bed in Kintalabad, refusing to budge from her side. He'd kept watch over her while she recovered from surgery, held her hand while she'd slept, soothed her when she woke up in pain.

He'd found it impossible to let her go. Every time he closed his eyes, his mind kept torturing him with the terrifying memories—that bone-chilling race through the canyon, the hunt for Singh's helicopter, the tense confrontation with his men—as Maya bled in his arms, her face so leached of color that he feared she'd already expired.

But he'd used the crown to convince Singh's men to help him. They'd made it to the hospital in time. And now her face had a healthier glow. Her shoulder was healing well. The doctors had removed the IV and taken her off the heaviest medications.

And the time had come for him to leave.

His gut churning, he took in her thick, dark lashes, the purple bruise fading to yellow on her cheek, and made himself acknowledge the truth. He couldn't draw this out any longer. He had no excuse to stay, couldn't keep putting his departure off. And he should leave now, before she awoke.

He didn't want to go. He loved her. He always had, always would.

But he'd seen the disgust on her face when she'd learned his identity. He was the son of her people's worst enemy, and he could never escape that fact.

Even worse, it turned out that she really might be the missing princess. She didn't know it yet, but the story was all over the news. Reporters had camped out in the hospital lobby. Security guards swarmed every floor.

And if it was true, her life would change dramatically. She would have duties, responsibilities—a far more glamorous life.

And she would have a family, people to care for her, just as she'd always dreamed.

A sad smile lifted the corner of his mouth. She'd make the perfect queen.

But he had no place in her royal life. She didn't need him, wouldn't want him. He would only remind her of all that was bad.

He rose, inhaled around the thick lump constricting his throat, took a final look at her face. This courageous woman had tried to sacrifice her life for his—after he'd failed her in every way.

Now he had to make this easy for her. He owed her that much. He couldn't let her down again.

His eyes burned, the pressure in his chest so massive, the yearning so fierce he couldn't breathe. Then he turned, strode blindly toward the door, willing himself not to look back.

It was the hardest thing he'd ever done.

He longed for her, ached for her, wanted her with a desperation he couldn't contain.

But for her sake, he opened the door and left.

Disoriented, Maya blinked at the sunlight streaming into the room. She took in the narrow hospital cot, the white blankets covering her legs, the gleaming, sterile floor. She pulled herself to a sitting position, stifling a moan as her bandaged shoulder twinged.

And then she remembered. Singh's gunshot. That searing blaze of pain. A helicopter. A plastic mask pressing over her face. Waking up during the night, seeing Deven sleeping in the chair beside her—his thick hair unruly, beard stubble darkening his handsome face.

She swept her gaze around the room, but Deven was nowhere in sight. A sudden fear made her pulse race. She couldn't have imagined him here. But where had he gone?

Someone tapped on the door, and her hopes rose. "Come in."

But instead of Deven, a young woman entered the room, followed by two large men. "Maya Chaudry?" the woman asked.

"Yes." Maya frowned, unable to place her. The woman was young, about her age, dressed in a T-shirt and jeans. And she was obviously Roma with her long black braid and sooty eyes.

"Do you mind if we come in?"

"No, but…" Maya eyed the two men with her. One was middle-aged, stocky, balding. The other was younger—probably in his mid to late thirties—ruggedly handsome and tall. He had a dangerous, rough-edged look.

But where was Deven? She peered around the visitors, hoping to see where he'd gone.

The woman stopped at the foot of the bed. "Oh, my." She slanted her head. "You look just like her. Doesn't she, Uncle Nicu?"

The middle-aged man stepped forward, and Maya shifted her gaze to him. He studied her for a moment, and then a tender look softened his face. "She's the spitting image."

Maya's confusion grew. "I'm sorry, I don't…"

"I'm Dara Adams," the woman said.

The name clicked. Maya's jaw turned slack. "The princess?"

"Well, not really." Dara's smile widened, and her dark eyes gleamed with delight. "Unless I'm mistaken, you're the real princess."

"What?" Maya gaped at her visitors. A laugh formed in her throat. "But that's crazy. I don't—"

"I should explain." The older man pressed his palms together in greeting. "I'm your uncle, Nicu Badis."

"My uncle? But—"

"It's a long story." He gave her an apologetic smile. "Do you mind if we sit down?"

"No, of course not." Suddenly dizzy, wondering if she'd lost her mind, she lifted a hand to her head. Could Singh have been right? Was she related to these people? But how could she be?

And where was Deven? She needed to touch him, feel his strength and support, find out his opinion on this.

The woman pulled up a chair. The younger man stood behind her, his big hand resting possessively on her shoulder. And suddenly Maya realized who he was. Logan Burke. The half-Roma man the princess had met in Peru—and eloped with a few months back. The tabloids had been full of the news.

Nicu took the chair on the opposite side of the bed. He leaned forward and cleared his throat. "I guess I'd better start from the beginning so it makes sense. The year you were born, Romanistan was in turmoil. Rebels were trying to stage a coup, and there were plots to assassinate our family. We tried to get the queen to go to England until you were born, to keep her safe, but she refused. And then she went into labor at the worst possible time. And she had complications. She nearly died."

"I brought a picture of her," Dara said. She opened a large, manila envelope, pulled out a photo and handed it to her.

Still not sure she wasn't hallucinating, Maya took the photo from her. The visitors watched her with expectant eyes.

She lowered her gaze to the picture, a professional portrait of the king and queen in their younger days—a wedding photo, she realized. The king wore a formal suit and flowered wreath, his handsome face beaming with pride. The queen was dressed in a red silk sari, adorned with golden jewels. Maya studied the woman's face, and the room began to spin.

The queen's face looked exactly like her own.

Her ears buzzed. Her head felt strangely light. She clutched the photo, wondering if she'd landed in another world.

"A bomb went off," Nicu continued. "Everything was thrown into chaos. We were afraid she wouldn't make it, that none of us would survive."

He palmed his bald head, tugged at the collar of his shirt. "Your father—the king—and I decided we had to keep you safe to protect the royal line. So I took you to a convent. We planned to keep you there until the danger had passed. I put the medallion with you for luck."

Maya tore her eyes from the photograph, too stunned, too overwhelmed to speak.

Nicu shook his head. "I had no idea what the medallion meant. None of us did. It was an old piece that had been in the family for generations, but the meaning had been lost. It was just a good luck charm—or so we thought."

Still incredulous, Maya found her voice. "I always thought it was lucky, too."

Nicu's smile turned sad. "Maybe not lucky enough. Bombs destroyed the convent. You disappeared. We were frantic, desperate. We searched the city, tore the place apart. Your father…he was beside himself. I've never seen a man so distraught. But we couldn't find you. We thought you'd died.

"We couldn't bear to tell the queen. She was so ill that no one believed she would recover. It would have been cruel to tell her the truth. We thought…we wanted her to die happy."

Dara leaned forward, a gentle smile touching her lips. "So they brought me in to take your place. I was an orphan."

Maya slowly shook her head, unable to absorb it all. It was like a television drama, certainly not real.

Nicu picked up the tale again. "The queen hadn't seen you yet—she'd had a Cesarean—so we thought we could pull it off. And then once she began to recover, we couldn't confess what we'd done. She was already so attached to Dara. And the Roma people needed hope. They needed to know that the royal line would continue. We didn't have the heart to break the bad news. But, Maya, you need to know…we didn't give up. We kept looking for you for years."

Maya jerked her gaze to Dara, then to the tall man standing behind her, still unable to process it all. "You're not joking?"

They shook their heads, gazing back at her with somber

eyes. She couldn't doubt their sincerity. They were telling her the truth.

"I... I don't know...this is all so bizarre," she said.

"I know," Dara said, sympathy lacing her voice. "I only found out the truth a short while ago myself. It takes some time to soak in."

Nicu closed his eyes, and when he opened them, Maya was stunned to see a sheen of tears. "I'm so sorry. All I can do is plead for your forgiveness. We did what we thought best—best for the queen, best for the people, best for you. But we ended up making a mess."

Maya's mind whirled. Her entire world had been turned on end. "If this is true..."

"It is," Dara said.

"Then I..." She shook her head, unable to absorb it. "I'd like to take a test. A DNA test. To make sure."

Nicu nodded. "Of course. But with the family resemblance, I don't think there's any doubt."

The family resemblance. The words jarred her, further detonating her life. This man was her uncle, the first member of her family she'd ever seen.

And suddenly, other implications roared in. Her family hadn't abandoned her. They'd loved her, wanted her, searched for her. And they'd put the medallion with her to protect her, just as she'd always dreamed.

She stared at the photo again—her parents, the people she'd longed to know—and blinked back a hot rush of tears. Everything she'd ever thought about herself had been wrong. She'd been wanted, loved.

"There's so much we need to tell you," Dara said.

Maya nodded, bit down on her trembling lip, too filled with emotion to speak.

"The crown is safe," Dara continued, tactfully changing

the subject, as if she understood Maya needed time to come to grips with the truth. "It's with the necklace and dagger. You'll need to decide what to do with them. Uncle Nicu will help."

"Singh's dead," Nicu added, a hard edge lacing his words. "We've confiscated his records. He had extensive lists of the members of his group, an entire genealogy. An international task force is rounding them up. The Order won't threaten anyone again."

Singh… *"Deven…"* Maya sat straighter. "Where is he? Did you see him?"

An awkward silence descended on the group. They glanced at each other, and Maya's agitation grew. "What happened? Where did he go?"

Dara's husband cleared his throat and spoke. "We saw him as we were coming in. On the roof. He was waiting for a helicopter to arrive."

"He's leaving? Now?" The blood drained from her face.

He hadn't stayed.

And without warning, the old insecurities flooded back, the sense of abandonment, rejection. The hurt. Deven hadn't cared enough, hadn't loved her enough to stay.

No, that wasn't true. Deven *did* love her. She'd seen it in his eyes, felt it in his kiss. He'd proven it time after time during their journey as he'd protected her from harm.

But he didn't think he deserved her. He'd even told her as much.

Her gaze landed on her newfound uncle, part of the family she'd always yearned for. Everything she'd ever wanted had just come true.

But none of it mattered without Deven. She didn't care about being a princess. It had nothing to do with her life. And she didn't need these people she barely knew.

She needed Deven. She loved him. She'd worn her independence as a mask to avoid getting rejected or hurt. But love required risk. If she wanted his love, she had to go after him and let her vulnerability show.

She swung down from the bed, disregarding the pain shooting through her bandaged shoulder. She had on a flimsy hospital gown, socks with rubber soles. She pulled a bathrobe from the foot of the bed and tugged it on.

"I'm sorry, I…I have to go."

"You're leaving?" Nicu sounded stunned. "But…should you be out of bed?"

Maya didn't bother to answer. She pushed past them, ignoring their startled faces. She had to find Deven, keep him from leaving. She just prayed that she wasn't too late.

She rushed to the elevators at the end of the hallway, her urgency mounting as she rode to the roof. The floors flashed by. The elevator dinged an eternity later and jolted to a stop.

She dashed out and ran to the double doors leading to the roof. She shoved them open and stumbled through, and was greeted by a deafening roar. Rotor blades throbbed. Cold wind blasted her face. She turned around, spotted the helicopter just as it lifted off.

And the man she loved flew away.

Chapter 16

Buffeted by the downdraft, the deep vibrations of the rotors pulsing through him, Deven watched the helicopter rise into the sky.

He couldn't do it. He couldn't walk away from Maya again. Even if she despised him, even if she refused to speak to him, he couldn't leave the woman he loved.

He shoved his hand through his windblown hair and watched the chopper shrink above Kintalabad's skyline, the noise receding as it headed toward the distant peaks.

He needed her, and maybe it was selfish, but he was going to beg her to let him stay. If she wouldn't have him, he'd just hang around in her periphery. Better to adore her from a distance than to never see her again.

He turned and started toward the double doors that would take him back downstairs. But then he spotted a woman standing across the rooftop with her face to the sky, her blue hospital robe swirling around her, her long, thick braid brushing her hips.

Maya. He stopped, suddenly unable to move.

She turned around as if he'd spoken, and their gazes met across the roof. Her face was pale, her eyes stricken. Her cheeks glistened with tears.

His lungs squeezed tight, sudden fear for her squeezing his throat. "What is it? What's wrong?" He hurried toward her, narrowing the distance between them, then stopped as close to her as he dared. He ached to hold her, pull her into his arms, but he didn't have that right.

She wiped her face with the heel of her hand. "They… They'd told me you'd left."

She was crying for him? He looked into her eyes, his heart faltering, hardly able to hope. "I tried to leave, but I couldn't go. I know I don't deserve you, but—"

"I love you."

"What?" He gave his head a hard shake, thinking his ears were still ringing from the rotors' noise.

She moved closer and placed her hand on his arm. "I love you, Deven. I always have. And I…" Her eyes glistened and brimmed with tears. "I don't want you to go. I need you."

She loved him. She needed him?

He wanted desperately to believe her, to seize what she offered, but he knew he had to be fair. "Maya… you might be the Roma princess. And if it's true, you'll become the queen. I'm Singh's son—"

"It doesn't matter. Your parents…my parents—none of that matters. We're still the same people we've always been."

"But—"

"You're the boy I fell in love with, the man I love now."

He lifted his hand to her cheek, his heart swelling, overcome by the emotions careening inside. "I thought I'd lost you that night. When you lunged for Singh…"

His throat knotted up. An unbearable tightness clutched his chest. And he couldn't resist anymore. He pulled her against him, careful of her injured shoulder, then enveloped her in his arms. He pressed her head to his chest, buried his face in her silky hair, remembering the blood, the fear, shuddering at how close he'd come to seeing her die.

"I knew it was better for you if I left," he confessed. "But I couldn't bring myself to go. I love you too damned much." He eased back, cradling her face with his hands, and gazed into her gorgeous eyes. "You really love me?"

A tear leaked down her cheek. "I always have. Stay with me, Deven."

He dipped his head and took her mouth, gently, tenderly, giving vent to the yearning he couldn't quell. He tasted her warmth, the sweetness of her kiss, the love.

An eternity later, he lifted his head. He traced the fading bruise mottling her cheek, so shredded by emotions he could hardly speak. But he had to be clear. He wanted no secrets between them, not anymore.

"I don't have anything to offer you. I don't even have a job. I resigned."

Maya's eyes searched his. "Your boss, Skinner. What happened to him?"

"He's been arrested." He let out his breath, still disgusted by the man's betrayal. "Interpol has Singh's records. They've started a worldwide crackdown on the rest of the Black Crescent group."

But there was more. "I'm Singh's only offspring, Maya. I inherited his estates, his wealth. But I'm not going to keep it. The money, the lands—it's all dirty. He got it from drugs, weapons, prostitution. I'm giving it away to charities like your shelter. To repair some of the damage he caused."

She smiled, a warm, gentle smile that soothed his heart. "I fell in love with you when you had nothing. And I still don't care what you own."

He framed her face with his hands. "Then you'll marry me? Even if I'm the son of your people's enemy?"

Her eyes gleamed. "Maybe it's time we changed history. We could merge the lines and start a dynasty of our own."

His heart missed a beat. "You'll have my children?"

"As many as I can. That's all I've ever wanted, Deven—a family with you."

Filled with joy, he pulled her carefully into his arms. And then he surrendered to the need sizzling inside him and kissed her—a deep, fiery kiss that incinerated every thought. Except one.

That he'd finally reclaimed heaven.

And this time, he wouldn't let her go.

Epilogue

"Almost ready, Your Highness?"

"Just about." Maya pressed her hand to her queasy stomach, struggling to hold down the soda crackers she'd swallowed minutes before. The ceremony was about to begin—her first formal function as queen, the long-awaited moment when they would formally present the sacred Roma treasures to the world.

And the last thing she needed was to get sick.

The maid straightened the hem of her sari and fussed with pleat of the skirt. The gorgeous gown had once belonged to her mother.

The queen. The edge of Maya's mouth ticked up. She still couldn't quite believe she was a member of the royal family. But there was no doubt. The DNA test had come back positive. She'd crash-landed into a fairy tale, going from orphan to queen.

The luxurious gown certainly made her feel like royalty.

Exquisitely crafted of red *zari* silk and gold brocade, it draped her like a dream. She wore her mother's heirloom jewelry— gold bangles on her arms, glittering earrings, rings on her fingers and toes. A jeweled *bindi* decorated her forehead. A tiny gold hoop graced her nose.

But all that paled next to the necklace Deven had given her on their wedding day. It glimmered against her throat, a shimmering mass of gold that never failed to make her heart catch. It wasn't his mother's lost heirloom, but it had replaced her medallion as her most precious possession, and she refused to take it off. She leaned toward the gilded mirror, eyed the red *sindoor* powder in the part of her hair.

She was married for real this time. And she thanked God every day for her good luck. Deven had been her rock over the past few months—hovering at her side, helping her adjust to the demands of her new life.

And they'd have even more demands to adjust to in seven months.

She pressed her palm to her belly, unable to stop the silly smile that kept threatening to erupt at the thought that she was pregnant. She couldn't wait to tell Deven the news.

"Here are your shoes." Gina—the young girl Maya had rescued a few months back—set them at her feet.

"Thanks, Gina." Maya stepped into the delicate sandals, then drew in a calming breath. "I think that's it. I'm ready to go."

She nodded to Gina to open the chamber door. Her role as queen was mostly ceremonial, but she still had influence— which she'd wasted no time wielding. The first thing she'd done was hire Gina, along with many of the other women she'd rescued, to make up her staff. She'd insisted that they continue to study so they could rise to more important positions later, either in the government or in schools. She intended to make sure all women in Romanistan got an education—and more power over their lives.

The door swung open. Maya headed into the hallway and heard the muted roar of the crowd inside the ballroom. Her nerves jangled even more.

Thousands of people had converged on the Himalayan palace for the event—royals, celebrities, antiquity experts, numerous heads of state. More people—Roma from around the world—crowded the streets outside.

And security was beyond tight. Antiterrorist experts had been called in from across the globe. An ant couldn't crawl near the palace without being picked up on a satellite somewhere.

She continued down the hall to the ballroom, the plush oriental carpet muffling her steps. The palace, which had once been Singh's, was now a museum of Roma history and heritage—starring the sacred treasures, of course.

Maya caught sight of Deven waiting by the ballroom door with her uncle. His broad shoulders filled his black tuxedo. His thick hair gleamed under the lights. He turned at her approach, and their eyes met. Her heart began its usual off-kilter sprint.

Would she ever get accustomed to this man?

She took in his freshly shaven jaw, the silver scar that had helped make him the man he was. Those eyes that promised ecstasy—and delivered it night after thrilling night. Not to mention the days….

His gaze lingered over her curves, making her heart gallop even more. His lips edged into a knowing smile, and his eyes took on a wicked gleam. "You look beautiful." He bent close, murmured into her ear, "How long until I can get you out of that dress?"

"Not long," she promised. She leaned closer, intending to

tell him her news, but the tall carved doors to the ballroom opened, and the tumult of voices drowned out her words. Resigned to waiting a little longer, she took her position between her husband and uncle.

The crowd hushed. Enormous chandeliers glittered overhead. They started across the thick Persian carpet toward the dais where the honored guests waited. At the front of the dais, the Roma treasures stood on display.

Maya's spirits lifted at the sight of the people she'd come to know in the past few months. On one side stood Dara, the former princess, Maya's adopted sister. They'd grown close as Dara had taught her what she'd needed to know. Dara beamed up at her handsome husband, Logan, the renowned mountain tracker Maya had met in the hospital. They planned to leave after the ceremony to return to Peru.

On the other side of the dais stood the couple from Spain— the sexy *gitano* thief-turned-security-expert Luke Moreno and his talented wife, Sofia, famous for her fabulous antique reproductions and restoration work. Heavily pregnant, Sofia still managed to look elegant in a plum-colored sheath, with her blond hair in a sophisticated twist. Luke gazed down at her, looking besotted. No one could miss the fierce love in his eyes.

Maya's uncle moved to the side of the dais. Deven stayed beside her as they took their places in the center of the group.

The crowd quieted. Anticipation hummed in the air.

Maya glanced around the crowded ballroom, filled with pride and satisfaction, then down at the treasures on the black velvet stand. To the right was the necklace, its meticulously hammered gold gleaming like fire. Beautifully crafted, it was adorned with symbols and tiny bells, rare amber that dazzled the eyes—black, green, red, a rare translucent blue.

The dagger was on the left. Over a foot long, made of patterned wootz steel, the lethal blade flashed as it caught the light. It had blood channels etched down the sides, a gold hilt big enough to fit a warrior's hand. The scabbard lay beside it—intricately beaded, embroidered with gold and silver threads in ancient Roma designs.

And between the dagger and the necklace lay the fabled crown. Her pulse quickened at the sight. It shimmered like the priceless treasure it was, a masterpiece from ancient times—solid gold, carved with the sun, the crescent moon….

A deep sense of awe consumed her. These treasures had endured for centuries. They'd fueled legends, fear, wars. People had hunted for them, died for them, murdered for them. And she could feel their magic, their power. They vibrated with unseen forces, truly a gift from the gods.

Her gaze traveled to the silver medallion—the piece she'd worn next to her heart since birth. And the sadhu's translation of the ancient inscription flashed through her mind: *both darkness and light provide insight into the heart.*

She inhaled and pressed her palm on her belly again. The Roma had seen their share of darkness. Her people had been conquered, persecuted, forced to wander homeless for too many generations to count.

But these treasures had given them hope, restoring dignity to a downtrodden people, instilling some badly needed pride. The Roma had begun to heal. Maybe that was the light.

Her eyes returned to Sofia and Luke, Dara and Logan, the people who'd helped fulfill the legend—now her family. Her gaze rested on Deven, her husband, and sheer happiness brimmed inside. They'd all journeyed into the heart of danger, then emerged from their own personal darkness into the light—the light of love.

A new era had begun for the Roma, and a new life was starting for all of them.

And speaking of new life… Maya scooted closer to her husband. "Deven…I'm pregnant."

His jaw turned slack. His startled eyes met hers. And then his shock gave way to the most exuberant grin she'd ever seen.

Unable to contain her own smile, she clasped his hand, feeling his warmth, his strength. His love. And then she turned back and beamed at the crowd. Thanks to the treasures, she had found what she'd always yearned for: love, the true power and the light of the world.

* * * * *

Don't miss Gail Barrett's next thrilling story!
Zoe Wilkinson only has hours left to rescue her famous
grandfather—and stop a deadly terrorist attack.
Running into ex-love Cooper Kennedy just as the clock
starts seriously ticking is a complication she doesn't need.
Their old attraction is more potent than ever—and it just
might be their greatest threat….

Look for
MELTDOWN
On sale May 2010
Wherever Silhouette Books are sold

Harlequin offers a romance for every mood!
See below for a sneak peek
from our paranormal romance line,
Silhouette® Nocturne™.
Enjoy a preview of REUNION *by* USA TODAY *bestselling*
author Lindsay McKenna.

Aella closed her eyes and sensed a distinct shift, like movement from the world around her to the unseen world.

She opened her eyes. And had a slight shock at the man standing ten feet away. He wasn't just any man. Her heart leaped and pounded. He reminded her of a fierce warrior from an ancient civilization. Incan? She wasn't sure but she felt his deep power and masculinity.

I'm Aella. Are you the guardian of this sacred site? she asked, hoping her telepathy was strong.

Fox's entire body soared with joy. Fox struggled to put his personal pleasure aside.

Greetings, Aella. I'm the assistant guardian to this sacred area. You may call me Fox. How can I be of service to you, Aella? he asked.

I'm searching for a green sphere. A legend says that the Emperor Pachacuti had seven emerald spheres created for the Emerald Key necklace. He had seven of his priestesses and priests travel the world to hide these spheres from evil forces. It is said that when all seven spheres are found, restrung and worn, that Light will return to the Earth. The fourth sphere is here, at your sacred site. Are you aware of it? Aella held her breath. She loved looking at him, especially his sensual mouth. The desire to kiss him came out of nowhere.

Fox was stunned by the request. *I know of the Emerald Key necklace because I served the emperor at the time it was created. However, I did not realize that one of the spheres is here.*

Aella felt sad. Why? Every time she looked at Fox, her heart felt as if it would tear out of her chest. *May I stay in touch with you as I work with this site?* she asked.

Of course. Fox wanted nothing more than to be here with her. To absorb her ephemeral beauty and hear her speak once more.

Aella's spirit lifted. What *was* this strange connection between them? Her curiosity was strong, but she had more pressing matters. In the next few days, Aella knew her life would change forever. How, she had no idea....

Look for REUNION
by USA TODAY *bestselling author Lindsay McKenna*
Available April 2010
Only from Silhouette® Nocturne™

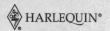

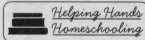
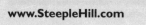

Silhouette® Desire

OLIVIA GATES

BILLIONAIRE, M.D.

Dr. Rodrigo Valderrama has it all…
everything but the woman he's secretly
desired and despised. A woman forbidden
to him—his brother's widow.
And she's pregnant.

Cybele was injured in a plane crash
and lost her memory. All she knows is
she's falling for the doctor who has swept her
away to his estate to heal. If only the secrets
in his eyes didn't promise to tear
them forever apart.

Available March wherever you buy books.

Always Powerful, Passionate and Provocative.

HARLEQUIN® Romance®

ROMANCE, RIVALRY
AND A FAMILY REUNITED

THE BRIDES *of* BELLA ROSA

William Valentine and his beloved wife, Lucia, live
a beautiful life together, but when his former love Rosa
and the secret family they had together resurface,
an instant rivalry is formed. Can these families
get through the past and come together as one?

Step into the world of Bella Rosa
beginning this April with

Beauty and the Reclusive Prince
by
RAYE MORGAN

Eight volumes to collect and treasure!

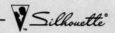

SPECIAL EDITION

**INTRODUCING A BRAND-NEW MINISERIES
FROM *USA TODAY* BESTSELLING AUTHOR**

KASEY MICHAELS

SECOND-CHANCE BRIDAL

At twenty-eight, widowed single mother
Elizabeth Carstairs thinks she's left love behind
forever....until she meets Will Hollingsbrook.
Her sons' new baseball coach is the handsomest
man she's ever seen—and the more time they
spend together, the more undeniable the
connection between them. But can Elizabeth
leave the past behind and open her heart to
a second chance at love?

FIND OUT IN

SUDDENLY A BRIDE

*Available in April
wherever books are sold.*

REQUEST YOUR FREE BOOKS!

2 FREE NOVELS
PLUS
2 FREE GIFTS!

ROMANTIC SUSPENSE

Sparked by Danger, Fueled by Passion.

YES! Please send me 2 FREE Silhouette® Romantic Suspense novels and my 2 FREE gifts (gifts are worth about $10). After receiving them, if I don't wish to receive any more books, I can return the shipping statement marked "cancel." If I don't cancel, I will receive 4 brand-new novels every month and be billed just $4.24 per book in the U.S. or $4.99 per book in Canada. That's a saving of 15% off the cover price! It's quite a bargain! Shipping and handling is just 50¢ per book in the U.S. and 75¢ per book in Canada.* I understand that accepting the 2 free books and gifts places me under no obligation to buy anything. I can always return a shipment and cancel at any time. Even if I never buy another book from Silhouette, the two free books and gifts are mine to keep forever.

240 SDN E39A 340 SDN E39M

Name	(PLEASE PRINT)	
Address		Apt. #
City	State/Prov.	Zip/Postal Code

Signature (if under 18, a parent or guardian must sign)

Mail to the **Silhouette Reader Service:**
IN U.S.A.: P.O. Box 1867, Buffalo, NY 14240-1867
IN CANADA: P.O. Box 609, Fort Erie, Ontario L2A 5X3

Not valid for current subscribers to Silhouette Romantic Suspense books.

Want to try two free books from another line?
Call 1-800-873-8635 or visit www.morefreebooks.com.

* Terms and prices subject to change without notice. Prices do not include applicable taxes. N.Y. residents add applicable sales tax. Canadian residents will be charged applicable provincial taxes and GST. Offer not valid in Quebec. This offer is limited to one order per household. All orders subject to approval. Credit or debit balances in a customer's account(s) may be offset by any other outstanding balance owed by or to the customer. Please allow 4 to 6 weeks for delivery. Offer available while quantities last.

Your Privacy: Silhouette is committed to protecting your privacy. Our Privacy Policy is available online at www.eHarlequin.com or upon request from the Reader Service. From time to time we make our lists of customers available to reputable third parties who may have a product or service of interest to you. If you would prefer we not share your name and address, please check here. ☐

Help us get it right—We strive for accurate, respectful and relevant communications. To clarify or modify your communication preferences, visit us at www.ReaderService.com/consumerschoice.

SRS10